Trevor K...

Prai...

C000053565

BAD DRE... REFLEC...IONS

Trevor Kennedy, Northern Irish editor of the widely acclaimed *Phantasmagoria Magazine* is a man of many talents... *Bad Dreams and Reflections: A Collection of Weird Horror Stories* published by Dark Owl Publishing LLC is yet another example of a creative mind that refuses to back down from any challenge...

Kennedy creates horror to perfection, a mad scientist just waiting for the lightning to strike... Kennedy [also] writes with a mournful pen, ink-stained future projections of a race too far gone to be saved.

This dark collection delves into the unspeakable injustices of those who devour all, and leave nothing but the deepest scars behind... a string of dark words, the coming together of many apocalyptic threads, a spider that weaves mankind's epitaph, one cautionary tale at a time.

- Jessica Stevens, peer review

In his introduction, Trevor Kennedy calls himself "something of a connoisseur of horror at its finest and most exquisite," which is a level of modesty I must disagree with.

The Crypt Keeper is a connoisseur of horror; curating and disseminating horror that only stodgy, busy-body parental groups could find objectionable. What Trevor Kennedy is, along with the likes of John Carpenter, Ramsey Campbell, and Robert W. Chambers, is a font of horror: a source from which macabre, terror, suspense, and dread flows.

When one finds Trevor Kennedy's work, it gives the same thrill of finding an unassuming book in a local small bookstore—the kind that ends up exploding the imagination out into tendrils which wrap around realms the reader never knew were missing from their life.

With the likes of "Relating to Thaumaturgy" and "The Crimson Tower," being part of the horror scene in Northern Ireland around about now will be viewed in the future as drinking in the same bars as Edgar Allan Poe, or being in correspondence with H.P. Lovecraft. I've been privileged enough to work, however distantly, with Trevor Kennedy for several years now. Even though we're thousands of miles away from each other, I can chart out how knowing him, and, even more, reading what he has written and what he finds important to read, has improved not only my writing skill, but, more importantly, enriched my life as a reader of the horrific.

~ Carl R. Jennings, author of *Just About Anyone*

All the stories contained within are set in Ireland, with some definitely falling into the strange category. Some of the stories are short and feel like little fever dream snippets... Where this collection shines is with the longer stories, all of which are creepy in their own right. "Crown of Thorns," which includes the genuinely scary character, Mr. Needlesticks, is the best of the bunch for me. ...there are more than enough excellent stories in here to make this collection worth reading. 4 stars out of 5.

~ John Watson, Horror Book R&R

Right from the introduction you get a good sense of how enthusiastic Kennedy is about horror. He states in his own words his life-long fascination with horror, and in particular H.P. Lovecraft. In fact, his first story, "The Cats of Silverstream," starts with the Lovecraft quote. It is a strange tale of a ghostly girl and a feline wail. But in no way does it set the tone for the rest of the book. Kennedy's writing morphs from eerily disturbing to dark comic satire to shocking. My favourite style of his writing is the dark comedy. This is executed to perfection in the story "So the Story Goes..." Having heard Kennedy's voice on his radio show, it was easy for me to read (in my head) this with a Norn Irish accent like Kennedy's...

It is fair to say that throughout *Bad Dreams and Reflections*, Kennedy's tone to each story changes. This gives the reader a real roller coaster of a read. I admire Kennedy's tongue-in-cheek humour, as much as I admire his ability to twist the story and deliver a shock when you least expect it. I also really enjoy the pace of his writing. As I read each story it became my new favourite until by the end of the book, I could not pick a favourite. Kennedy has a talent to deliver every time and can turn his hand to any number of narratives...

I look forward to reading more of his work in the future.

- Helen Scott, peer review

BAD DREAMS AND REFLECTIONS

A Collection of Weird Horror Stories

by

TREVOR KENNEDY

From
Dark Owl Publishing, LLC

Arizona

Cover image by ofjd125gk87 from Pixabay
Cover design by Dark Owl Publishing

Visit us on our website at:
www.darkowlpublishing.com

Also From

Dark Owl Publishing

Collections

The Dark Walk Forward
John S. McFarland

The Last Star Warden
Volumes I and II
Jason J. McCuiston

The Last Star Warden:
The Phantom World
Jason J. McCuiston
Available only on Kindle

The Last Star Warden:
The Crimson Star Saga Episodes
Jason J. McCuiston
Available only on Kindle

No Lesser Angels, No Greater Devils
Laura J. Campbell

The Tension of a Coming Storm
Adrian Ludens

The Nightmare Cycle
Lawrence Dagstine

The Art of Ghost Writing
Alistair Rey

The Brotherhood of Secret
Darkness and Other Cults, Cabals,
and Conspiracies
Jason J. McCuiston

Welcome to Scar Ridge
Jonathon Mast
Coming October 2023

Anthologies
A Celebration of Storytelling

Something Wicked This Way Rides

Novels
The Black Garden
John S. McFarland

The Mother of Centuries
The sequel to *The Black*
Garden
John S. McFarland

The Keeper of Tales
Jonathon Mast

Just About Anyone
Carl R. Jennings

The Malakiad
Gustavo Bondoni

Carnivore Keepers
Kevin M. Folliard

The Wicked Twisted Road
D.S. Hamilton

For Young Readers
Annette: A Big, Hairy Mom
John S. McFarland

Grayson North,
Frost-Keeper of the Windy City
Kevin M. Folliard

Shivers, Scares, and Goosebumps
Vonnie Winslow Crist
The sequels are coming soon!

Buy the books for Kindle and in paperback
www.darkowlpublishing.com

*Dedicated to Dave Carson, John Gilbert, and Stephen Jones,
without whom I wouldn't be doing what I'm doing. Thank you!*

*And to my biggest supporter, my mother Doreen,
and my niece Margot Haywood:
for when she's old enough to read (horror)!*

TABLE OF CONTENTS

INTRODUCTION:
REFLECTING ON BAD DREAMS

There are two main types of horror for me, both equally as important and staples of my own lifelong fascination with the genre.

There's the profound, serious stuff that resonates deeply within our very bones, forcing us to examine and look right into the very core of existence itself—to bring into question and challenge what we believe to be reality. If done right, it leaves us awestruck, blown away by what is presented to us by the author or filmmaker, tattooing an indelible mark on our minds and souls, that *comforting* uncomfortable feeling that we have experienced something very special indeed. Perhaps even a little peek behind the curtain of Creation itself, the briefest of glimpses at the mechanics of the *unknown* Universe. Think of the works of Howard Phillips Lovecraft, Montague James, Robert Aickman, Ramsey Campbell, and David Lynch, all of whom were, or still are, geniuses and artists in their respective fields.

I'm not even talking about "horror" or "fear" in the popular sense of the words here. No, these are the types of works that I would very possibly describe as an intellectual, creative *thrill*—a buzz that no drug or drink could ever replicate, although this feeling is not easy to do justice to with mere words. If, however, like me, you are something of a connoisseur of horror at its finest and most exquisite, you will understand what I mean.

Then there's the really fun stuff that I would describe as "ghost train" horror and which I adore just as much as the aforementioned. I'm talking ghoulish, rotting hands suddenly popping up from below the earth of a spooky old cemetery to drag you down, screaming, into its nightmarish, spider-web-infested underground lair. Or perhaps vampires and werewolves running amok, biting the necks and ripping out the innards of their unsuspecting victims, in need of a good bloody staking or silver bullet through the heart! Cursed tomes (Lovecraft again?) and ancient demons with nothing but the very nastiest of intentions on their malevolent, Hell-dwelling minds. You get the picture—*The Evil Dead*, Hammer, and all the rest.

Yes, of course, there are many, many other subgenres within our field, but for me, the above two are the most important and my greatest loves. It is also most certainly my intention that this is reflected in some small way through the following stories that you are about to read—some new, alongside others that I consider my strongest over the last decade or so, perhaps collectively in their own way my personal and respectful tip of the hat to that which has influenced me for as long as I can remember.

There's a little of myself in there at the same time—places and people inspired by real life and such. The title of this collection is also a nod to one of my other main points of reference: my own literal nightmares and recurring dreams, especially those from when I was in a very dark place in my life and would experience regular nighttime visions of Hell and black drapes with strange, indecipherable runic etchings on them. I still haven't worked out what those damned curtains and symbols mean!

I'd also like to confirm, in reference to the story "The Evil Men Do: A Warning to the Self-Indulgent"—because I have seriously been asked this before!—that I've *never* actually murdered anyone, or even planned or attempted to! The idea for that one came when I asked myself what the worst thing imaginable would be to wake up to after an alcoholic binge and blackout.

I hope you enjoy the tales collected here. I've tried to balance the seriousness with (hopefully) a few laughs thrown into the mix. I also hope that for you non-UK-based readers my use of Northern

Irish vernacular and slang at times doesn't alienate you or ruin your reading in any way. I'm sure you'll get the references and—all being well—appreciate what I'm trying to do with this love letter of sorts to the horror field.

So, with thanks to you, dear reader, and to editor and publisher Andrea of Dark Owl for having faith in this book in the first place.

Trevor Kennedy
Belfast, Northern Ireland
April 2023

THE CATS OF SILVERSTREAM

It is said that in Ulthar, which lies beyond the river Skai,
no man may kill a cat; and this I can verily believe as I gaze upon him
who sitteth purring before the fire. For the cat is cryptic,
and close to strange things which men cannot see.
He is the soul of antique Aegyptus, and bearer of tales from forgotten
cities in Meroe and Ophir. He is the kin of the jungle's lords, and heir to
the secrets of hoary and sinister Africa. The Sphinx is his cousin, and he
speaks her language; but he is more ancient than the Sphinx,
and remembers that which she hath forgotten.
- H.P. Lovecraft, "The Cats of Ulthar"

The wail of a cat is a dreadful sound. I think it is even more disturbing because it sounds so similar to that of the cry of a baby, immediately conjuring up worrying thoughts of an infant in trouble. Many a night I have lain in bed, unable to sleep due to the wretched screams that the felines in my street have directed at my house, their continuous, cacophonous caterwaul of catastrophe drumming through my mind, as if they were consciously, sentiently, attempting to drive me over the edge.

Or perhaps they have been trying to warn me of something? An omen maybe, a harbinger of bad tidings.

Why were there so many of them that would gather? And why only at night, after the daylight hours had quickly been enveloped by the oncoming darkness and its unholy secrets? I fear I may never know the answers to my questions as I now take refuge in the mountains of Cavehill, barely still human, barely sane...

It was late afternoon last Thursday. Autumnal leaves were sweeping through my street in a gentle October breeze, freshly fallen from the almost skeletal trees, Hallowe'en approaching.

I'd finished my work for the day and had decided upon a nap before having my dinner. I was lying on top of my bed with the window open, listening to sounds of the outside world in the street below, feeling myself drifting off, when I heard the crying. It was different from what it was before, however. It didn't sound like that of a cat, or even a baby, more like a child. At first, I thought it was nothing to concern myself with—probably just kids being kids—but it continued... incessantly.

I got up and looked out the window. Dusk had settled but I could make out the figure of a young girl, aged about eleven, wearing a red dress and standing in the shadows at the corner of the street. She was hiding underneath some trees, her hands covering her face, audibly but softly weeping—clearly upset or in some form of distress.

I wanted to help her but was apprehensive at the same time. Where were her parents? Why had no one else come to her rescue? Why was the street now deserted? Had I fallen asleep, now dreaming?

A moral obligation made me rise from my bed and go outside to try and aid her.

As I approached, the child's cries intensified. I nervously, gently placed my hand on her shoulder and asked what was wrong.

The girl removed her hands from her face to reveal the physical embodiment of a nightmare. Her eyes blazed deep crimson: behind them, Hell itself resided. Her mouth opened to greet me with large, razor-sharp fangs which she hastily sank deep into my throat.

As I collapsed to the ground in shock and piercing, trembling pain, I noticed that the mysterious cats of the night had begun to gather 'round the scene, watching intently, silently, contentedly. Gleefully. At first there were just a few, then dozens of them arrived, their sleek, silk-like fur black as the night itself.

As panic set in all I could do was flee.

I haven't stopped fleeing since.

I've been hiding on the Cavehill for a few days now. I'm very sick, hungry, and my throat is badly injured. I think I may have completely lost my mind.

I can hear something approaching, its wails echoing in my ears.

It sounds like the cry of a baby.

SKULL & BONES

A mist had formed, slithering along the damp street, snaking in and out of the barren trees that lined the footpath. It was not quite day and not quite night as the streetlamps feebly attempted to illuminate the way ahead for Allan. Were those chestnut trees that lined the footpath? Oaks? Nature never had been his strong point.

Allan sensed he had been walking for a very long time. Or perhaps no time at all. Possibly days, potentially seconds. *Years?* He knew where he was; he just didn't know how he'd gotten here. He couldn't remember anything really, not properly. He knew his name and who he was—sort of—but everything else was patchy at best.

Allan continued walking. At least he knew what he was approaching.

As Allan reached the end of the street, the shop came into view on the other side of the main road. That old shop. He knew it meant something special to him, but he couldn't quite recall what. It had a welcoming air of familiarity, like reacquainting with an old friend after many years, not much having changed. Even the neon purple sign above the door spelling out THE CANDY BOX and the dim, somewhat faltering light inside seemed to be greeting him, welcoming him back—the prodigal son returning home at last.

Allan smiled, a warm feeling trickling inside of him. *Is this what nostalgia feels like? Where did that word come from?* He couldn't remember.

Crossing the main road to get to The Candy Box would be easy as there were no cars speeding up and down it. Of course there weren't. There were no cars and no motorbikes and no people and no dogs and no cats and no birds and nothing at all, really. Just the road and the shop. Or so Allan thought.

The Candy Box. Allan's old friend from some unknown period in his past, here to reconnect with him. But why? He crossed the road, nonetheless. A spider, about the size of a bus, scuttled down the road silently behind him. Allan didn't notice.

As he stood in the open doorway and the neon sign above his head crackled and flickered, Allan heard faint whispers coming from the direction of the back of the inside of the shop, but no one could be seen. Was this an echo from a previous time? An era now long ago? What was this place? What was it *really*?

A thought suddenly struck Allan, a fleeting, returning memory now hammering home in his consciousness: Arcade games. Poker machines. Flashing lights. Computerised graphics. *Ding, ding, ding—you've hit the jackpot!*

The back of the shop was where the arcade machines were kept, a place Allan and his friends had spent many a happy hour as teenagers. He just had to go and look. To find out for himself.

As Allan walked through the desolate shop, a giant cockroach perched on the ceiling watched his every move, staring intently, malevolently, *inhumanly*.

Have you ever wondered what goes on behind the eyes of an insect? Ever *really* thought about it? It's not pleasant, not pleasant at all. It's dark in there, so very dark. Dark and malicious. Hell and chaos in their purest forms.

The huge insect slipped silently across the ceiling, curiously following Allan into the back shop.

The machines were there waiting for him, switched off, frozen in time, as if silently, patiently, longing for attention. *Street Fighter II* was there, as was *Bomb Jack* and the gambling machine with the electronic playing cards. More memories came flooding back to Allan: Playing *Street Fighter II* against that kid Daffy who lived around the corner (the little shit always won, beating all the older boys at it!), winning £15 from the gambling machine—a lot of money for a lad back then! *Wasn't I also a paperboy?* thought Allan.

Allan fancied a go at *Street Fighter II*, for old time's sake, but after checking his trousers' pockets he realised he had no money on him. He switched the machine on at the main socket anyway.

No luck. It was as dead as the proverbial doornail. He tried the plugs for the other machines. Same result. But if the electric was down, then what was powering the outside sign? Allan decided to go outside and check.

As he walked back through the shop, past the rack with the videotapes, Allan suddenly thought of the TV that would sit above the shelf beside where the tape cases were. He looked to the side of the rack and there it was by the far wall, just as it had always been. Allan walked over and switched the television on.

It spluttered into life—somewhat, anyway. Interference, white noise. Voices, whispers, unintelligible. It sounded like someone was in deep distress, crying out for help. Were they talking backwards?

The noise seemed to be growing in Allan's head, slowly becoming unbearable, like a blunt kitchen utensil scraping through his mind whilst a needle prodded and poked and played around in it. He attempted to turn the volume down, but it only seemed to worsen. He couldn't take it anymore and quickly changed the channel.

Children's music. He recognised it instantly. A soothing, melodic tune that reminded him of his pre-school days, an innocent time of wide-eyed wonder. It was beautiful and the polar opposite of what had just come before. As Allan listened to the calming, sweet music, an oversized woodlouse sat on top of the shop counter and looked on.

What had begun as a mesmerizing novelty was quickly descending into a terrible nightmare as the repetitive children's music went on and on and on, getting louder and louder, all throughout the shop, and now mixing with the backwards-talking insanity and cries of anguish from before. Allan was quickly losing his grip on what was already a rather delicate grasp of reality. He ran out of the shop in confused horror.

Allan stood outside the bastardised version of The Candy Box and struggled to compose himself. Was this a panic attack coming on? A nervous breakdown? Death itself? *Am I already dead?* he mused. Moments from his life—stolen memories perhaps, those which up until this point had been missing—suddenly shot back into Allan's mind: as a young boy walking down the old stone path to school with his friend Jonny; playing football with his mates on the playground; as a teenager hanging around the very shop he was now standing in front of—or at the very least, a twisted, fucked-up recreation of it; holidays to the caravan with his parents and brothers; dabbling in drugs and alcohol; his first girlfriend; his grandfather's death when he was eighteen; his first job in the factory which he hated; going off the rails whilst intoxicated... They weren't all good memories. Some of them were bad ones. *Really* bad ones. The *worst*. The *awful* things he had done.

Across the road, a thin man in a dirty grey shawl beckoned to Allan, attempting to grab his attention. He was bald with no apparent eyebrows or lashes and hand gaunt, skeletal features, including elongated fingers which pointed in Allan's direction, seemingly reaching right across the road to pull him along with him.

When Allan finally noticed him, so great was his confusion and numbing fear he felt he had no other choice but to cross the road and see what the man wanted. A large abomination, something akin to a ladybird fused with a centipede, followed Allan as he crossed the road.

"Come with me. I have something very special to show you," grinned the bony man in an accent Allan could not quite place. Together they walked in silence further down the road, the ladybird/centipede travesty retracing their steps but keeping its distance, now also joined by the cockroach from before. Allan felt like he was living in a deeply unsettling dream, expecting to wake up any moment now, but this didn't appear to be happening.

"I know this road but can't remember its name. What is it? Shankvale? Woodhill?" enquired Allan of the bony man.

The bony man just grinned again and didn't speak. They continued to walk side by side, passing shops and houses that looked like they hadn't been populated in millennia.

The bony man eventually stopped at the stone steps of an imposing black building and pointed at its wooden front doors, inviting Allan to enter.

"What is this place?" asked Allan.

"It is a library," replied the bony man.

"What type of books does it stock?"

"The most important ones."

"I don't remember this place being here before. There was a library on the road, yes, but this is not it."

"It has always been here. You just haven't noticed it before."

"What's inside it? What do you want to show me?"

"Why, a book, of course," said the bony man, grinning even more so now, his odd, white, almost featureless face appearing to be relishing the moment.

"What book?"

"*Your* book."

"What are you talking about? That doesn't make any sense. Where am I? What is this place?"

"Are you telling me you don't know where you are? You have been here long enough. Tens of thousands of years, in fact."

"Who are you?"

"Depending on your definition of the term, I am God. At least to someone like you, I am. I am *your* God now, and within those doors awaits your judgment. You can put it off as much as you like, but you cannot avoid it completely. You were but a man, alas a weak-minded, base animal, but a creature of certain sentience, nonetheless. The rules must be obeyed in full. Together we must read your book."

"Am I dead?"

"You are no longer living, if that helps."

"What are my options?"

"They will depend entirely on what is held within the pages of your book."

"I've done bad things in my life. I've killed someone."

"I know you have."

"Can I escape from this place?"

"It is not a common occurrence. Take my hand."

Allan looked around in despair, and for the first time since he got here, he noticed the over-large insectoid bastard offspring denizens of this netherworld—the detestable, unspeakable pets of the bony man. Multitudes of them had now gathered around the library:—giant beetles, worms, spiders, cockroaches, and more, many of them fused together. Some even had wings and were hovering high above the ground. Behind their dead eyes and antennae and blank expressions, there appeared to be a consciousness, an *intelligence*. A collective consciousness perhaps, a hive mind. And what were those strange clicking noises? *Click, click, click, clack, clack, clack.* Were they speaking? Were they muttering amongst each other? What were they saying? They seemed to be excited, gleeful. They were enjoying the spectacle, reveling in it.

Allan wept as a small child would. He no longer had a choice.

As he turned away from the hellish sight in front of him and placed his hand in that of the bony man's, Allan now saw him—no, *it*—in its true form. It wasn't just thin, it wasn't just bony; it *was* bones, its visage a blank, emotionless skull with deep, dark empty sockets where its eyes should have been, behind which resided a bottomless abyss of forbidden, twisted secrets and knowledge.

Together, hand in hand, the entity and Allan walked through the doors of the strange library as the ever-expanding sea of monstrosities behind them watched on and pleasurably clicked and clacked.

SO THE STORY GOES

*T*he story, as it goes, begins at Half Moon Bay, in the charming and postcard picture-perfect seaside resort of Shannon in Northern Ireland. County Antrim, to be a little more precise. In addition, the events depicted in this anecdote are all completely true, partly true, or not true at all. It happened quite recently as well. So, let us waste no more time and familiarise ourselves with the ripping yarn of Andy and Daphne's first and final date together.

Uncle Paulie's Ice Cream Emporium, which was situated right on the seafront, could be best described as looking more like a 1950s American diner than an ice cream shop, complete with a retro jukebox playing contemporary pop songs—the perfect spot to hold a jitterbug contest. The attire of the staff also matched this era. However, this was just part of its charm. It was a well-run and friendly place, popular with the local teenagers and somewhere for them to hang out that didn't involve underage drinking and/or recreational drug use, although a whiff of weed could often be smelt from around the side of the business, and yes, this was also the same area where various grubby sexual encounters had occurred over the years, too. The shop itself served many confectionery treats of an ice-creamed nature, but the jewel in its crown was undoubtedly its succulent whipped ice cream. I mean, regular ice cream is good, but that of the whipped variety is the dog's bollocks. Not literally, of course, but you just cannot beat a whipped ice cream poke (as we like to call it here in Northern Ireland) with a flake and nuts on top, and Paulie's were arguably some of the best on the planet!

Paulie Esposito himself, who was naturally of Italian descent (his father heralded from the old country, settling in Shannon after meeting, falling in love with and marrying a local girl in the 1940s), was a greasy, rotund man in his fifties. Amicable in nature, Paulie had taken over the family business after his papa, Haitham, had passed away from a heart attack in 1994. He, too, married a local girl, named Alice. Remarkably, Paulie was not unlike that other Uncle Paulie in appearance—the one from the 1990 Martin Scorsese gangster film, *Goodfellas*, played with a classy and sinister grace by actor Paul Sorvino. Our Paulie, however, thankfully had no connections to the Mafia or organised crime. At least not that we know of, anyway.

On this particular night in question, so the story goes, twenty-one-year-old Andy was sitting in the pink-themed ice cream parlour waiting on his eighteen-year-old date, Daphne, to arrive. She was ten minutes late and Andy was beginning to feel that he was being stood up... once again, by a girl. Andy had often seen Daphne around the town and in the DVD rental shop where she worked nights. She had always seemed a little strange to him, but there was something rather intriguing and mysterious about her at the same time. Plus, she had the most amazing red curly locks, huge, deep green eyes that you could almost fall into, and a body to die for.

Andy eventually got talking to her one night when he was returning *Batman vs. Superman* to the shop; the movie was actually quite an enjoyable blockbuster, despite the critical panning it received when first released in cinemas. Lex Luthor, played by Jesse Eisenberg, was a hoot! Anyway, they got chatting, tedious small talk really, with Andy quite enjoying Daphne's candour and directness. He soon had a "fuck it" moment and asked her out for an ice cream, despite already having a long-term girlfriend whom he was somewhat getting bored of and now felt he needed a fresh "challenge." Daphne agreed to meet him on Tuesday evening, her night off, which was also Hallowe'en night, incidentally. Andy was delighted and even reckoned that his luck could be in on the night in question, if you catch my drift. He was certainly going to give it a try, as he reckoned the confidence she exuded and the revealing outfits she wore made her a probable goer.

Andy was about to give up the ghost and make tracks for home when Daphne arrived in a very relaxed and chilled-out mood, apparently unconcerned at her poor punctuality. She didn't even apologise for being late. Andy let it go because his date was wearing a very revealing, almost hypnotic, black top, displaying quite a bit of her more-than-ample cleavage. This somewhat aroused and distracted Andy. The usual air-kissing nonsense and social niceties were exchanged, before Andy went to the counter and ordered Daphne's choice of treats from Paulie's wife, Alice—a tub of mint choc chip and a can of Fanta lemon. Andy had a whipped ice cream 99er and a Coke.

They soon got down to the serious business of idle chit-chat when Andy returned, putting their mobile phones away whilst David Bowie's majestic apocalyptic classic "Five Years" crooned from the jukebox. The end of the world had never sounded so good!

Andy was boring Daphne with talk about himself (he was a bit of a self-obsessed and egotistical bore, after all, but a generally decent spud when all was said and done) and his work in Belfast as a semi-skilled factory operative in Collage Digital Colour, a printing factory. He was discussing the tedious details of his car journey to and from the factory when Daphne decided enough was enough and cut in to begin a discussion about her own favourite topic: films. Specifically, horror films.

"So, do you watch films much? I know you hire the odd DVD out at the store, but what would your favourites be, then?" she began.

"Not big into movies, to be honest, love, but don't mind those superhero and *Fast and Furious* shows. I'm big into my cars, you see," retorted the disinterested and slick-haired Andy.

"Cars don't impress me. Usually, guys who are obsessed with their precious motors are just posers trying to make up for the fact that they have tiny dicks."

This both shocked and gobsmacked Andy.

Daphne continued, "Anyway, I'm not saying you're like that, but I prefer my guys to be a little more cultured, if you know what I mean. I do like my nights out to the theatre and am a big film buff too, but none of your all-action, big-budget Hollywoodised shit either. I prefer the films of David Lynch, classic horrors like *The Exorcist* and *The Shining*, and some foreign films."

"Ugh! I hate movies with subtitles and black-and-white ones. Such pretentious nonsense, and too hard to follow as well. Never even heard of yer man, Martin Lynch," exclaimed the philistine that was Andy.

"David Lynch!"

"Whatever. I've no time at all for that sort of arty shite. I don't mind the odd vampire film though. Those *Twilight* films were pretty good."

"Are you for fucking real, mate? Those films are pure cack and so are the books, and I've read them all, by the way! The acting is wooden, the plot is flimsy at best, and since when did vampires become sparkling, lovesick tweens anyway?"

"I liked them and the girl who starred in them—Kirsten or Bella or something—was pretty hot too."

"No way. Those films are truly awful and based on shite books too, just like that *50 Shades* of whatever crap. And anyway, vampires should always be cold-blooded, evil, murdering bastard sons of monsters to me, not cute pinups that resemble David Beckham. It's ridiculous. We need to go back to how vampires were originally depicted in the early myths and legends. The best vamp films were in the 1970s and '80s, before Buffy—and to a lesser extent that *Interview with the Vampire* film in 1994—made them all sexy, sympathetic, and relatable. It actually makes me want to vomit. We need more Christopher Lees and fewer Robert Pattinsons. Real vampires must be spinning in their undead graves at these great insults to their species! Is it any wonder they hate and have nothing but contempt for humans?"

Daphne's ferocity and passion amused Andy greatly, and turned him on a bit too, as Batimora's "Tarzan Boy" emanated loudly from the jukebox speakers.

"You don't look or dress like a Goth or emo girl, but I can see you are very enthusiastic about vampires. You do know there's no such thing as them though, right, ha, ha? And don't even hit me with those silly blood-drinking rumours connected to the murders last month on the edge of the woods. That was obviously the work of some escaped lunatic with a big knife or the like, hence the cutting up of the body parts."

"Then how do you explain the bite marks found on the victims' necks?"

"That was never proven; those are just old wives' tales, for want of a better phrase. There's no such things as vampires, ghosts, or goblins. That's a scientific fact, so it is. Anyway, what's your favourite vampire movie of all time, then?"

"As I said, the older ones are by far the best, going back as far as Max Schreck as *Nosferatu* in 1922. Christopher Lee is also the quintessential Dracula to me, but Bram Stoker's original novel is the best of the lot, as most, if not all, book versions are. The stuff at the beginning, set in Castle Dracula, is some of the greatest Gothic literature I have ever had the pleasure of reading. But, yeah, I'm a big fan of '70s and '80s vampire and horror films. It was such a golden age for the genre. We had classic vamp flicks back then like *Texas Chainsaw Massacre* director Tobe Hooper's *Salem's Lot*, based on the book by Stephen King, *Near Dark* with Bill Paxton and Lance Henriksen, Romero's *Martin*, and of course, *The Lost Boys*, which perfectly balances the comedy and horror, just like *An American Werewolf in London* did a few years earlier. *Fright Night* was a joy to behold, too. The recent remake was naturally a big pile of steaming dog turd, with David Tennant being the only good thing about it, although I may be a little biased in that department. Out of the current batch of vampire films, most of them are pure shite, but the best and most realistic one would have to be the Scandinavian flick, *Let the Right One In*. Vampires have always been my favourite. Always."

"You know your stuff, love, I'll give you that, but to be honest, I've never even heard of most of those films."

"Why does that not surprise me?"

"I thought a girl like you would have been more into chick flicks and American high school comedies. Do you not like those?"

"To me, those sorts of films are complete and utter fucking donkey's balls and an insult to one's intelligence! Does that answer your question?" she asked, before adding, "You think you're a real smooth ladies' man, don't you, Andy?"

"Well, I can be a real beast in bed, you know?"

"Yea, well I'm not like other girls, so don't bother getting your hopes up, Mr. Cool Dude. You hear me?"

They both laughed, making intimate eye contact and enjoying each other's company despite their obvious differences. Daphne also chose to ignore Andy's irritating naming of her as "love."

They chatted a while longer, mainly about where they liked to go for nights out and such, with the generally agreed feeling that local club Xanadu was long past its best but was still okay for a cheap night out. When a few kids dressed as a witch, Yoda from *Star Wars*, and SpongeBob SquarePants walked past the window, on their way to presumably go trick-or-treating, Daphne lamented how Hallowe'en had become too commercialised due to the influence of American culture, and that it should return to its pagan and mystical roots. A good example of the rape and pillage of this ancient Celtic festival was, as she pointed out, the silly decorations ordaining the walls and windows of Paulie's Ice Cream Emporium. Daphne sighed. Andy didn't really know what she was talking about, but nodded his head in agreement anyway.

After a second helping of ice cream-related snacks and soft drinks, Daphne told Andy it was time she headed for home, as it was getting late and she had to be up early in the morning for an appointment. Andy offered to walk her home, with an ulterior, sex-related motive. Daphne agreed, warning him that she lived alone on the outskirts of the town and it was quite a walk to her small flat, but they could take a shortcut through the woods beside the moors. Andy was more than happy to take whatever route Daphne pleased and the news of her having her own place made him even more eager, as he equated that this gave him even more of a chance of getting the leg over, the horned-up young whipper-snapper that he was.

They walked hand in hand through the town, on what was an unusually mild and dry Hallowe'en evening. Dusk was beginning to settle in the cloudy sky above and more young'uns passed by with their pumpkins in hand whilst dressed up as skeletons and comic book heroes like Spider-man and Iron Man.

As they were passing Xanadu, they happened upon local character and joker Michael Kane, who was his usual highly intoxicated and jovial self, his black curls stuck to his head by a drunken sweat. His eyes were as wild and crazed-looking as they always were. At this particular moment, he was being hassled by a couple of well-meaning male E-heads, obviously on their way to the Hallowe'en rave at the club. They were telling him how much they loved him and that he was a great guy, shaking his hand firmly and hugging him intensely. Michael's response to their compliments was a simple thrust of his hands up into the air and the shouting of, "Bullshit, lies, wankers!" before the parties headed in their separate directions. Daphne and Andy chuckled at this amusing encounter before moving on down the road, across the old moors and towards the edge of the woods, chatting away happily about this and that. It was nice and felt good and right, too.

"You know, these woods are pretty creepy, especially with it being almost dark. Please feel free to grab and cuddle me if you get too scared now," Andy jokingly stated.

"I'll keep that in mind, you big brave hero, you," responded Daphne sarcastically.

The moon was hanging in the sky, attempting to shine through the thick Hallowe'en clouds and mist which had fallen suddenly, to light a way for the couple as they reached the middle of the woods, arm in arm. The place felt alive with damp nocturnal wildlife, while a sharp chill cut through the air.

Daphne and Andy could now see their breaths in front of them, and soon Andy slipped on a wet fallen tree trunk while they were clambering over it, resulting in his becoming even more damp and cold. He really wasn't an outdoorsy type at all. Daphne, however, was, and definitely much more adept at the woodland terrain than her male counterpart.

As they approached and walked on to a more open greener area in the forest, Andy felt it was now the right time to make his move. He tugged Daphne's arm and pulled her around and towards himself, grabbing her by the waist tightly and squeezing his crotch area into her own for added effect.

"Giv'us a kiss, love, wud ye?" he demanded in a totally unclassy manner, before leaning in to get his snog and hopefully a bit of a feel.

But he was left kissing the air when Daphne broke free from his horny clutch and fell to the ground, screaming and writhing in agony, grabbing her head and ears by her hands.

Andy was panicked and did not know how to react, so he simply stood back and watched, feeling and looking rather useless, as his date for the night began to contort and increase the volume of her now high-pitched screams.

"*It's happening again! It's fucking happening again!*" she yelped in apparent extreme pain.

What happened next sent Andy completely insane. The switch in his mind simply flicked to "off," as you would do with a light switch perhaps, his panic turning to sheer fear-induced terror.

Before Andy's very shocked eyes, Daphne's arms, hands, and fingers extended, eventually becoming huge, animal-like, razor-sharp claws. Her ears also elongated, becoming pointed and growing hairs alongside others that were sprouting up all over her greatly stretching and pulsating body. The clothes the teenage girl had worn on her date, including her sexy black top, were soon ripping and falling off her now gigantic, masculine torso and onto the ground. The final part of her metamorphosis happened when her mouth area swelled and grew, revealing massive, pointed fangs in place of her previously quite petite and very human teeth. As her eyes rolled back inside her now beastly head, she produced two new bright yellow ones.

The creature formally known as Daphne then looked up at the full moon above and howled the lycanthropic base wail of a creature of the night.

The last thing Andy would ever see in this world would be an eight-foot-tall hulking monster hovering over him before it lopped off his head in one swift movement of its muscular right arm and claw, leaving his body to slump onto the ground motionless, aside from the large amounts of blood gushing from the part of his neck that remained.

The beast-creature that used to be an eighteen-year-old girl pounced animalistically after the human head it had just sliced off and grabbed it, holding it up to the moon like a trophy and howling repeatedly in a primal and terrifying screech.

That Hallowe'en night, the creature claimed many more innocent lives throughout the idyllic-appearing small town of Shannon, in a massacre that saw the body parts and internal organs of their victims devoured and mutilated beyond recognition, leaving behind a trail of guts and destruction.

Or so the story goes.

A TALE FROM THE CRYPT

Woman: *"Do you dig graves?"*
Neil the Hippie: *"Yeah, yeah, they're all right."*
Woman: *"I'm so glad. I think they're wonderful!"*
- *The Young Ones*, "Nasty", season 2, episode 3

*I*t's an old story, of course. Probably as old as storytelling itself. An urban legend. A myth. Variations of it told countless times before over the decades, maybe longer.

In a nutshell: Guy visits cemetery. Guy plans to grave-rob. Guy opens coffin lid. Dead dude in coffin jumps out and gives guy the fright of his life.

Predictable enough, I hear you holler. But not always...

The thing is, my version of the tale is true. One hundred percent, bonafide, no bullshitting, no exaggerating, fact. I was there, I should know. It's gospel. So it is written, so it did happen... and all the rest. So, here's my tale from the crypt, every last word of it a cold, hard, indisputable fact...

It was the 1980s. A glorious time of playing football in the street and terrorizing the neighbourhood with hijinks such as wrapping people's doors and running away and throwing stones and fireworks at their windows. Rubbish Aussie soap *Neighbours* was essential viewing (God bless that nosey old biddy Mrs. Mangle and Bouncer the dog!) whilst the crème de la crème of the British entertainment world was fronted by—at least those who *weren't* predatory, serial sex offenders such as Messrs. Savile, Harris, et al—such greats as the Krankies (long before schoolboy-dressing-drag act Jeanette became First Minister of Scotland), Timmy Mallett and his rodent companion Roland, and Pat Sharp, who adorned a rather fetching mullet in the Fun House.

Perpugilliam Brown was sending the pulses of young lads and bored dads alike racing in *Doctor Who*, as Zammo was taking hard drugs in *Grange Hill*. Keith Harris and a young Phillip Schofield were even making a fortune by sticking their hands up the arses of unsuspecting animals, while Michael Jackson was still black and had developed a blossoming relationship with a chimpanzee named Bubbles, for some reason.

Corporal punishment was still alive and well in the schools, and, long before the advent of the Internet, pornography had to be acquired by the discovery of a stray dirty magazine—more often than not with the pages suspiciously stuck together—in a hedge or derelict house, or by simply sneaking a sly peak at the bra section of your mum's Kay's or Littlewood's catalogues.

Splendid times indeed, but back to the main story...

Hallowe'en was fast approaching, and on a cold, rainy, and windswept Saturday afternoon, my mate Marc and I were bored out of our tiny little skulls as we sat in his bedroom twiddling our thumbs and contemplating a plan of action to relieve us of the tedium.

We were both aged fifteen, and despite it being the season of all things dark and mystical—when the dead themselves sneak a peek into our world for the very briefest of moments—it was just another miserable afternoon in Belfast with nothing to do. I suppose we could have gone to the nearby Ballysillan Leisure Centre and done something sporty and active for a change. But that required effort and money, something we, as bone-idle smelly teenagers, lacked in droves. We also felt we were too old to dress up for Hallowe'en and go around the doors singing and collecting money—no way, that shit was gay and for kids, not cool mother-fuckers like us.

So, as we watched Des Lynam discussing the football results coming in on *Grandstand* while the heavy rain pelted off the window, we considered renting out a video, but we'd already seen practically all the good horror and action films the shop down the street stocked, so that was now out of the question, too. They'd probably also refuse us a blue movie if we asked, so the idea soon petered out completely, along with others.

Boring, boring Saturday. Boring, boring, boring...

Suddenly a brilliant—and rather daring—idea popped into my head like a jack-in-the-box on amphetamines.

It concerned something that had been relayed to me by one of the older boys we were friendly with, Rick. Rick himself was something of a role model and hero of ours, never playing by the rules, man, a natural rebel who had no time whatsoever for the bullshit of the adult world. Rick was also an expert shoplifter, one of his tricks being to enter the best clothes shops in town while wearing a pair of dirty old jeans. He would then take a pair of the best and most expensive jeans—usually Levi's—into one of the changing rooms, try them on, then walk out of the store with the new pair still on and the old ones left back in the rack—genius in its simplicity, really!

Anyway, Rick had recently told me about an old, abandoned church up near Belfast Castle and the Cavehill. I knew the road he was talking about but had only glimpsed the old church, situated behind a row of houses, once or twice when driving past as a passenger in my dad's car. According to Rick, in his somewhat infinite wisdom, the church contained a crypt underneath it, where, back in the day, some rather well-to-do rich people had been buried, still wearing their expensive gold jewellery and rings. He told me he planned to go up there one night and help himself to their possessions, hoping to become extremely rich himself through it. When I questioned him on the somewhat sketchy morality of what he was planning—essentially grave robbing—he replied with: "Fuck 'em. It's not like their gold's any good to them now. The auld fuckers have been dead for years now anyway." And that was that, the argument settled in the most eloquent of terms.

Although I reckoned Rick may have been lying—about either the crypt or its contents, or both—the idea was now becoming more and more appealing to me. It was well dodgy, of course, and if we were caught, we'd no doubt get into a shitload of trouble. And what if Rick had gotten there first and raided the crypt before us? Or what if Marc said no to my mad idea? Would I even be brave enough to go up there on my own in the middle of the night to grave rob *actual* corpses in their coffins?

As it happened, Marc was just as morally dubious and morbid as I, so when I suggested the plan to him, he agreed straight away, believing it to be one of my best yet!

It was still raining when we sneaked out of our houses and met in the street at midnight. Marc was wearing his Nottingham Forest tracksuit, which his mum had bought him the previous Christmas. I always found it a little odd that a kid from Belfast would support that team, as most lads in Northern Ireland back then would support either Manchester United or Liverpool in England.

I was wearing jeans and a jumper and an Adidas tracksuit top; both of us were also wearing battered trainers that had seen better days, having kicked many a football on a muddy field or cinder pitch. Marc had also brought with him a torch, a hammer, and a flathead screwdriver from his dad's toolbox for the opening of the coffins of the rich dead dudes we were planning on robbing.

As we walked through our own area of the Ballysillan towards the Cavehill Road and its fabled, crumbling church, the rain eased somewhat while a thick mist settled upon the land, the full moon in the sky now barely visible, struggling to light our way ahead along with the faint orange glow of the streetlamps. We appeared to be the only two people alive in the area—or at least awake. Not even the usual sight of a stray drunk stumbling and mumbling home could be spotted. It was eerie and clichéd, like something from an M.R. James story, or a Hammer horror film, or maybe even that old series, *Tales from the Crypt*. All that was missing was the hoot of an owl.

When we arrived at the row of houses, behind which was the church, we were cold, tired, and a little hungry. We hadn't really prepared for our adventure, but bravado would not allow either of us to admit that to the other. We were certainly not bottling it and turning back, either—no chance of that!

As silently as possible, we climbed over the wall of the house closest to, and backing onto, the apparent front of the long-abandoned church, into the owners' front garden, stomping all over it, slipping round the side and into the back. To access the entrance to the church we had to pass through their well-kept back garden and across a small green with overgrown weeds and shrubbery. The grass in the back garden was long enough in and of itself, and by the time we'd reached the small field before the church—a building in complete disarray, falling apart—the damp had already soaked through our trainers and up to the bottom of my jeans and Marc's tracksuit.

Why was this old church tucked away so remotely here anyway? The houses had obviously not always been here, the church existing for many years before, probably decades, maybe even centuries. But why did it appear that the houses had been erected in such a manner that would *hide* the church away from public view? Why had it been abandoned? What happened here so long ago? I knew this part of the city very well—I'd grown up and been a paperboy in the general area—but why did I not properly know about the building's existence, only glimpsing it in passing a couple of times? It didn't really make proper sense, an ancient hidden church like this slap-bang in the middle of North Belfast. What type of church was it? Protestant? Roman Catholic? Something else altogether? Something that predated the aforementioned?

Now standing with the building right in front of us—towering over us arrogantly with malevolent intentions, perhaps?—we were both clearly apprehensive about entering it. Our silly little idea of grave robbing seemed just that, *silly*, but once again our bravado in each other's presence forced us to move forward anyway, towards the church's wooden and rotted front door, which lay open, beckoning us in.

The exterior of the building was grand in scale, Gothic in appearance. Odd gargoyles surrounded the spire on top, creatures the likes of which I had never witnessed before, and certainly not as part of the decoration of a church. Tentacled, ugly abominations, fish-like, inhuman monstrosities. Denizens of some unknown, dastardly plane. The rest of the building was shrouded in mist and overgrowth; where once stained-glass windows would have sat proudly, now the frames were windowless, the wind breathing cold life through the empty spaces into what was presumably a dank interior.

When we entered what appeared to be the front entrance, above the rotten old door was a carving of another of the horrible fish-like tentacled creatures, below it an inscription in some form of indecipherable etchings and language, jumbled up letters impossible to make sense of in an apparently nonsensical, random order, some perhaps even missing or eroded over time:

Cthulhu R'lyeh

Inside, the main church was laid out in the shape of a cross, but over the resulting years, and after working out the exact bearings of it with a compass and other tools, I have come to realise that it appears to have been shaped in the manner of an *inverted* cross. There was nothing but mess all around with a sinister, putrid odour hanging in the air. Bird droppings, dead insects and small rodents, debris and what apparently appeared to be blood were strewn across the floor and even covered the walls in part. There were no pews, just more and more of the mess, the only sound to be heard presumably that of a bird (a bat?) flapping somewhere in the dark of the high ceiling above us. Shadows all around were playing tricks on us.

In front of us was the church altar, but one unlike we had ever seen. As we walked up the four steps of the blackened altar, we were greeted by a centrepiece statue that we couldn't fully make out before getting closer. It portrayed a majestic and daunting creature of immense power, which I have no doubt it both commanded and received. Horned on top and tentacled at the mouth, it carried in its left hand a great sceptre; on its head was placed the most regal of crowns. Below the statue was an inscription yet again written in that unidentifiable alien tongue.

As Marc and I studied the inscription trying to make some sense of it, I noticed a trap door in the ground, just at the foot of the unholy statue. It was easily opened—as if something was wanting... *inviting*... us to discover its presence. Although anxious and afraid of what was beneath it, I slowly opened it anyway and was greeted by a set of stone steps leading downwards. It obviously led down to the crypt Rick had told me about—the one with the coffins and the corpses and the gold rings and the rich dudes' jewellery. Despite an obvious fear now residing deep within the both of us, Marc switched on his torch, and we walked down those cold stone steps.

"Let's get this shit over and done with and get the fuck out of here as soon as possible. This place is giving me the right creeps," stated Marc as he approached the first coffin he could find in the dusty old cobwebbed crypt, which contained at least seven of the long wooden boxes.

"Fuckin' right, mate. I don't even give a shit if we find anything worth stealing here anymore," I responded.

At first, Marc tried to prise open the lid of the coffin with the flathead screwdriver he had brought with him, the torch resting on top of it, but it wasn't budging despite his best efforts. "Well, are you not going to help me?" he snapped.

I didn't say anything in reply, feeling both helpless and afraid. Marc just shook his head, placed the torch on the ground, and took to the coffin violently with the hammer, raining blows upon the lid of it, blow after exasperated blow until finally, the wood cracked a little.

Marc turned and smiled at me in morbid glee before bringing the hammer swiftly down upon the coffin again and again.

CRACK with the hammer! *CRACK! CRACK! CRACK!*

The wood of the old coffin splintered completely, bursting the lid open to reveal its contents to those who dared to look. When Marc looked inside, his face quickly changed from a look of frenzied determination to one of confusion, then to sheer abject horror.

The inevitable happened next...

A withered, skeletal claw, its skin hanging sloppily off the bone, suddenly reached up and viciously grabbed Marc by the back of his hair, pulling him swiftly down towards the open coffin. Marc let out a loud and desperate scream as he was dragged down. I ran over, shocked and trembling, and attempted to help my friend any which way I could, only to be greeted by the sight of a wide-eyed face from the very pits of Hell itself biting deeply into that of Marc's, gnawing greedily with its rotten teeth into the cheek and nose of my best mate, before casually tossing him aside and sitting up straight in the coffin, staring at me with menacing intent as a long, slithering centipede crawled out of its left eye socket.

What I did next was in a state of total and utter panic. I am not proud of it, and it still haunts me to this very day.

I fled for my life, leaving my apparently unconscious friend behind me to meet his fate. I could try to justify it to myself by claiming I ran to get help, but that would quite simply be a lie. In truth, I ran because I was completely terrified. I ran because I was, and still am, a coward, one who has never since been able to properly face the dark of night, with all its dark and terrible secrets.

But that is not the end of my story, which, in all honesty, would indeed have been a rather predictable one. There are a couple more twists to the tale, which I shall relay to you now.

Just before I ran for my life on that fateful night, I grabbed hold of Marc's torch—I knew I needed it to find my way out of the crypt and up those stone steps in the dark. As I bent down and hastily clutched the light from the side of the coffin, I couldn't resist a final look at the horrible *thing* that had risen, and when I did, that was when the *true* shock hit me. I knew the cadaver had looked somewhat *familiar* but couldn't quite put my finger on it. It was quite small in height, not like a fully grown man and most certainly not that of an *old* man. It looked more like the rotting corpse of a young teenage boy. As I raised the torch in the direction of where the dead body was sitting up in its resting place, that is when the full realisation of what I was looking at hit me—it was wearing a Nottingham Forest tracksuit!

The last thing I remember before running from that crypt screaming like a lunatic was glancing at the inscription on a plaque on the wall just above the coffin. This is what it read:

HERE LIES MARC DARREN LAWTHER
FIFTEEN YEARS OLD
DIED SUDDENLY OF FRIGHT
CURIOSITY AND GREED KILLED THIS CAT

When I got home and woke my parents, raving like a mad thing, they eventually calmed me down and had me taken to hospital by ambulance. Whilst there, I was told that I had had some sort of complete mental breakdown and, on top of that, had never really had a friend named Marc Lawther, either. In fact, no one of that name and age even lived in Northern Ireland—I had simply invented him, a figment of my own rather vivid imagination, having ventured out that night with no one but myself. They also informed me that no church of the description I had given them existed in the area.

When I was eventually released from care, my first port of call was, naturally, to Marc's house. At first, I was greatly relieved when his mother answered the door—I wasn't mad after all!—only to slip back into profound disorientation and confusion when she informed me that she didn't have a son named Marc and was, actually, childless and that I should stop trying to pull cruel pranks on her.

I headed straight for the old church in the Cavehill area behind the row of houses, only to be greeted by a plot of empty wasteland. It was as if the Universe was playing an elaborate, twisted joke on me.

It's now 2022 and Hallowe'en is approaching again. I've replayed that night of my childhood many times in my head over the ensuing years, over and over and over again. I've now come to the conclusion that I am completely sane and all of it really did happen, and I really did have a best friend named Marc Lawther in the bargain. I believe I owe it to him to keep his memory alive.

I still can't explain what happened, however. Did I become caught up in some sort of time loop? A parallel dimension maybe? Was Rick somehow in on it all? He's still knocking around and still maintains he visited the church, too, perhaps now being my only reliable witness. Is Marc still out there somewhere, or did that cursed church or *something* deep within it erase him completely from existence?

It's all still a great, perplexing mystery to me, and one I fear I may take to my very own grave when the time comes.

One thing I do know for certain is that for the last thirty-plus years, I feel like I've become the main character in a fucking David Lynch film. And that's not something I really want to be.

IT BEGETS

A man is born alone and dies alone; and he experiences the good and
bad consequences of his karma alone;
and he goes alone to Hell or the Supreme abode.
- Chanakya

Somewhere in Belfast, 1997

The book dropped gently from the man's hands and fell onto the floor of the squalid living room of his ground-floor flat.

He had fallen asleep in a drunken stupor again, this time fortunate he didn't have a lit cigarette in his hand, risking dropping it from his brown-stained fingers, just like before, the ensuing blaze put out hurriedly by a neighbour passing by who had just happened to notice what was going on in the nick of time. It had been a lucky escape. And not for the first time.

Luck always runs out, however.

The book he had been reading—or at least attempting to in his inebriated state—was a second-hand copy of Mark Twain's *The Mysterious Stranger*, which he had been given recently by his nephew. The story concerns the nephew of Satan, who pays a visit to a small town in Austria during the Middle Ages where he causes some, well... *devilment* towards three young boys and the neighbouring villagers.

This type of tale was not the man's usual fare as he generally didn't like supernatural fiction, but the parts that intrigued him most were the musings on the plight of man and how despicable a species humankind really is, inferior in morality to the rest of the animal kingdom, despite an intellectual superiority. This had resonated profoundly with him. He had witnessed firsthand his fellow human beings—including his comrades in arms—at their most reprobate, their most base. Unspeakable acts of malevolence committed against innocents whose dying pleas for mercy went ignored as their families screeched in abject terror.

But all these barbaric violations against everything that is good and decent were mere slim pickings when compared to his own foul deeds.

He didn't believe he was an evil man, or at the very least, not born evil. Perhaps just a foolish one who had committed the vilest of acts. One who from an early age had given up on his own dreams and aspirations to fight for "The Cause," brainwashed as an impressionable youth by Fagin-type bullies with sinister agendas, the same so-called heroes who never really believed in The Cause in the first place and would later sell out when the chips were down and money and further power were on the table.

But what of the foot soldiers who had sacrificed so much? Simply discarded and cast off like the proverbial pieces of shit on the shoe of life that they were. It was a bitter pill to swallow. As horrendous as his own crimes had been, they were committed for the sake of a much grander plan and a brighter future for his children and his children's children.

However, the man had always had a dark shard buried deep within his soul, an appetite that regularly needed whetting, longing to be satiated. Like the addict who so desperately craves his fix.

As the man drifted into a deeper sleep, he dreamed the dream of the guilty. That recurring chimera where he spoke to his many victims in the flesh, begging with them—screeching desperate orisons to whatever god or gods might exist out there—for forgiveness. But the gods always remained silent, their hands resolutely covering their ears.

The young boy was up first, just as he always was, the first victim. The fifteen-year-old mentally handicapped kid—the "retarded spastic" as they had jokingly referred to him—who had been accused of telling the wrong type of tales to the wrong type of authorities. The man and his associates had dragged the boy away from his screaming mother, bundled him into the boot of a car, taken him away to a remote spot in the countryside and shot him point-blank in the head. They had dumped his young and broken body in the waste ground beside the old zoo, a blatant disregard for the preciousness of life, just as a fly-tipper would casually discard an old fridge or shopping trolley.

It was the man himself who had pulled the fateful trigger that night.

The young woman was next to appear. The twenty-five-year-old blonde whose breasts he had sliced off in the back of his old Ford Escort with a stolen butcher's knife. Her crime, her reason for being "selected?" She had simply been born into the wrong religion. Such was the fate of many during the period.

The married couple and their nine-year-old daughter then stepped forward, their faces still brutally charred from the Christmas Eve blast that had claimed their—up until then—happy lives so prematurely, the bomb in the shop having been planted by the man just before making his cowardly escape in his co-conspirator's getaway vehicle.

All the man's victims simply pointed at him accusingly, their bleak faces locked in a combination of anger and sadness, condemned to eternity in the unknown ether, trapped in Limbo until the score is settled and their souls finally freed.

The dream—just like it did every time—then suddenly changed. The man found himself in a hallway illuminated by black candles, flickering gently in a calm but always heavy and sinister air. At the end of the hallway was a set of majestic black curtains created from the richest of materials, not of the world of the living. Adorning the drapes in bright, finely crafted gold lettering was a series of indecipherable symbols, ancient runic etchings from a time long, long forgotten.

The man studied the intimidating curtains for what may have

only been a few seconds, or perhaps even several million years. In Hell, time does not flow in the same manner as it does in the natural world.

Despite never wanting—but always feeling compelled—to, the man once more walked through the regal drapes towards what lay in wait for him, and always had done since the beginning of the Universe itself, countless millennia ago. His ultimate fate.

The Court was, in human terms, akin to the Colosseum in Rome—perhaps these ancient peoples had based their stadium on it, after their own flirtations with the gods of old. But the Court was much more magnificent in terms of size and scale, with a ceiling that appeared to stretch up towards Heaven itself. The countless—almost infinite—rows of seats were formed in a circle and occupied by a variety of differing beings, all gathered in their own groupings, perhaps kept apart for reasons known only to them.

An atmosphere of sheer dejection encompassed the entirety of the place.

To the left and right sides were the former humans, the victims—*every single* victim that had ever lived and breathed on Earth, their faces contorted permanently in a never-ending rage as they furiously spat out curses and insults towards the man.

In the front and back rows were what appeared to be angels, the most beautiful of beings that ever existed. But on closer inspection, due to the look of a most terrible despondency upon their visages, it was clear that these were indeed the Fallen Ones, those brave but foolhardy beings who had at one time dared to question the wisdom of Solomon and the Supreme One on his throne.

Standing in the centre of the Court was an infernal nameless being. It is believed to be literally impossible to utter his true title in the human tongue, so *inhuman* it is. The Nameless One's attire was a simple black, hooded cloak, made, it appeared, from the same rich material as the entrance curtains to the Court, complete with similar runic symbols. The being's countenance could be—at times anyway—briefly glimpsed at as that of a man's with very handsome, well-drawn features, and the most intense, piercing eyes imaginable, burning with a fierce fury, on fire with a wicked vengeance. Perhaps he was the *original* Fallen One? At other times, depending on when and how you looked upon it, its facial complexion took on a very different appearance—that of a skull, the space inside its empty eye sockets reaching right down into the chasms of eternity itself, an abyss of its very own, one that had witnessed many terrible events. In its arms, The Nameless One held a book, a tome written long before humanity ever coughed and spluttered its way into existence, before the stars had ever formed in the sky.

Before even attempting to plead his case for forgiveness, the man, frozen to the spot and whose last remnants of wit were slowly slipping away forever, was judged guilty by the baying crowd of lost souls as they once again taunted, insulted, and spat in his direction. The Nameless One simply admired the spectacle in front of it before slowly stepping up to the man and whispering a single word in his ear in an elegant tone unlike any he had ever heard before—"*Amen.*"

At this prompt, the crowd of lost souls broke free from their seats and made haste in the direction of the man, the eternal multitudes clambering over and fighting with each other to get at him with nothing but a determined, unfathomable rage set deep within their dead eyes and anger-filled, broken hearts...

The man awoke screaming and sweating profusely, in the very same way he had done the first time he had the dream many years before, and something he had continued to do every single time he had experienced it afterwards. He reached over to the messy ashtray on the table beside him and checked through it for a decent-sized butt. When he found a passable one, he lit it and sat back on the 1970s-style, stained, navy blue chair where he had just slept and sighed, contemplating his next move.

The shakes were in the post, so he knew he would have to get more vodka and cigarettes soon to delay them for at least another day. He'd probably have to phone the taxi place again that delivered during the night. Despite the nightmares, the vodka—which he took with ice when he could even be bothered—helped him sleep and take his mind off things. He certainly wasn't one for bars or company and preferred to do it alone.

He didn't consider himself an alcoholic—a problem drinker maybe—as alcoholics to him were those losers and wasters who sat on park benches and pissed and shat themselves whilst vomiting into the top pockets of their shirts. No, he reckoned he was much more strong-minded than that; plus, it greatly relaxed him. He had often mused that his nightmares could be the result of his regular heavy drinking (that's all it was to him—"heavy"), a mild form of delirium tremens perhaps. But he had also experienced them during long periods of abstinence too, so it remained a mystery. He put these thoughts temporarily out of his mind and pulled himself up off the chair to grab the remainder of the near-empty bottle of vodka on the other side of the room by the window before phoning for more.

Stumbling across the room, the man's bones ached. He glanced at his reflection in the mirror above the fireplace. He wasn't a young man anymore, his best days far behind him, his mop of grey hair, thinning face, and wrinkles a far cry—a shadow—of his former glories as the good-looking, charismatic smooth-talker who in his prime had bedded more women than he'd had hot dinners. An old man now, nearing the twilight of his existence, bones creaking as he moved like the stereotypical wooden door in a haunted house. He'd lost some weight too, he'd noticed as he looked at the ribs that showed beneath his skin from the open, raggedy shirt he had been wearing for a few days now. He looked away from the man he almost didn't recognise in the glass and moved to the window where the bottle sat.

It was a clear night outside, the bright moon above making the visibility even clearer as the trees at the back of his flat danced lightly in the gentle breeze. The stars almost resembled that famous Van Gogh painting, such was their vitality. It was the sort of view that reminded him so much of the happier times when he was a boy, fooling around outdoors at all hours, getting up to a multitude of innocent larks with his friends. Back before everything changed. Before the bad times. Before the tragic loss of said innocence. Was he a victim of circumstance, the era in which he was born, or would he have always ended up as a "wrong 'un" anyway?

As the man went to bend down to pick up the bottle of alcohol, he noticed something else in the trees that quickly grabbed his attention. He saw some rustling in the shrubbery, some mild commotion within the woods. Someone was out there. No, not someone, but several people.

The man's first thought was the obvious one to someone who had lived a life such as his in a country such as this—it was the "other side," come to settle the score once and for all. Something which had happened countless times before—men with woolly faces armed with guns made in faraway lands, tit for tat the order of the day in this small corner of the world. It could be kids fucking around however, he mused. He really *hoped* it was kids, but he was taking no chances and had been prepared for such an eventuality—as this could very well be—for many a year now. He might have been well past his best, but he still thought of himself as a hard man, not to be fucked with and about to prove that point once again in the harshest of terms. Did they know who he was? Did they *really* know?

Summoning what strength he had remaining, he quickly pulled the 9mm Browning from under the cushion of the chair that he had just been sleeping in and made for the kitchen and the back door.

Ducking down below the window in the door, he quietly and slowly opened it, more anxious than he had been in quite some time. Peeking through the crack where the door lay ajar, he looked out in silence.

Nothing.

The trees and growth several yards from him swayed easily in the wind.

Easily but almost *knowingly*. Sinister, even.

Keeping to the left side, the untrained "soldier" quietly sneaked towards where he'd noticed the earlier movement, being as gentle on his feet as was humanly possible, hoping upon hope that the element of surprise would work in his favour and not to the fortune of his enemies.

He soon reached the wooded area, and with a bold rush of blood to the head he broke the silence, attacking the branches desperately with one arm, his loaded handgun cocked and readied in the other.

But there was nothing there. *Nada*. Not a peep.

It had all been a wild goose chase.

The man knelt on the ground and sighed deeply, breathing heavily into the night in a combination of exhaustion, embarrassment, and sheer relief.

He remained on the ground and thought to himself for what felt like a very long time but was really only a few minutes.

Was he imagining things now?

Maybe he was clinically paranoid.

Perhaps he really was experiencing the heebie-jeebies.

It was at this point that the man was grabbed violently from behind by the hair and dragged deeper into the woodland, the gun slipping from his hand like a child dropping a toy. He let out a squeal like a trapped animal before being hauled around to face his destiny.

The faces before him were both ghoulish and familiar.

They were all there, of course. Every one of them.

The handicapped kid. The young blonde woman. The married couple and their daughter.

Their expressions were blank yet determined at the same time. They stared at him in a sombre, almost regretful and sad silence, but also content with the knowledge that they were going to do what they had come to do.

It *had* to be done.

The man knew this, too.

His victims didn't strike him; they didn't have to—he was

paralysed with shock and fear; the rest was now inevitable. He didn't even put up much of a struggle when they pulled him into the shallow pit in the earth that they had prepared for him.

It was almost as if the man was now—no, not at peace...—*accepting* of his final punishment, as they dumped him into the makeshift grave.

As the man's victims threw handfuls of dirt onto him from above, he didn't even scream as he looked up at the last faces he would ever see in this world. He simply sobbed and regressed to his childhood, pleading for his mummy.

The man closed his eyes as the soil and muck rained down on him, into his mouth and nostrils, choking him, making him cough and gasp for air in a weak and feeble panic.

His final mortal thoughts before the darkness enclosed him were ones of remorse for a life that had resulted in so much wrong being inflicted upon the innocents, direct violations against the natural order of things.

But it was too late for all of that now.

The man came to in a hallway illuminated with black candles. There was a thick, heavy atmosphere all around. He knew he had been here for an amount of time but wasn't quite sure exactly how long. It may have been a few seconds or even minutes. Or perhaps a billion years. It was hard to tell.

Ahead of him, just as he had expected, were the majestic black curtains, speckled with the strange runes. Usually, he would walk up to the curtains himself before entering what lay beyond. But not this time. This time there was a figure there to greet him, to *welcome* him home.

The cloaked figure with the face that flickered between that of a beautiful angel and one of a bony-faced abomination took the man by the hand, and together they passed through the curtains and into the Court.

Where the souls of infinite victims waited patiently.

"The fact that man knows right from wrong proves his intellectual superiority to the other creatures; but the fact that he can do wrong proves his moral inferiority to any creatures that cannot."
- Mark Twain

Dedicated to the memory of all the innocent victims of the Northern Ireland "Troubles."

A CACOPHONY OF VOICES

*T*he young woman sat alone on an old wooden chair in the filthy room, the mysterious envelope placed neatly on her lap. She lit up a cigarette and eyeballed her surroundings.

The house was an old terraced one in the Shankill area of West Belfast. Technically she owned the house, as Peter, her estate agent husband, had acquired it some weeks prior with the intention of renovating it before renting it out. She had pinched the keys from her other half's office earlier that morning when she called in to see him on the pretence that she just felt like rewarding her hardworking sweetheart with a well-deserved sandwich. A chicken and mayo sandwich it was, too—his favourite.

The interior of the Battenberg Street home was in some serious ruin. The 1970s-style brown and yellow patterned wallpaper was ripped throughout, stained, and adorned with graffiti, while at some point the living room ceiling had caved in. Some Robin Hood-style cheeky chappies, presumably local men, had apparently cleared the empty house of anything of value, including the copper wiring, radiators, and carpets, since the previous elderly owners were long since gone, the wife having passed away and the widower husband now residing in a nearby care home. The debris of empty bottles and cans of alcohol along with joint roaches appeared to be the work of local youths who found somewhere to crash.

The woman was extremely apprehensive about opening the envelope. She could have opened it at home, but she didn't want to expose her two young daughters to whatever essence its inside may have been holding. If what she was told was true, then its contents could quite possibly bring a great curse upon her, but she was also profoundly intrigued by it, maybe even obsessed.

Since she was a small girl, she had always had a great interest in all things occult-related, the mysterious. As a teenager, she regularly played on a Ouija board with her best friend, Laura. The board had been given to the woman as a child by her maternal grandmother, who oft claimed to be a witch who could make contact with the deceased, but the silly old dear was never taken quite seriously by anyone at all.

Laura and she did everything together after becoming close friends when they met in their very first year of primary school. They sat beside each other in school for twelve years, liked the same pop stars, and shared their deepest secrets about boys together. "Here comes trouble now" and "the terrible twins" were just a couple of the things people would say whenever they saw them together. Their October birthdays were only a week apart, and their first jobs were the same as well, working together in the HCL call centre in town.

Tragedy struck when they were twenty-one, however, after Laura collapsed during a rave at a nightclub named Xanadu situated somewhere in the countryside. Laura had been taking illegal substances at her best friend's behest, never regaining consciousness, and was officially pronounced dead a few hours later at a nearby hospital.

It was a grey, overcast day outside, looking like it was about to pour with rain at any moment. From the small front window, the woman could see and hear some boys in the street playing football, joking and laughing with each other. *They better not hit my bloody car with that ball!* she thought to herself, overprotective as always of the flashy, expensive sports car her rich husband had presented her with a year prior as a random gift for the love of his life.

She looked at the envelope situated on top of her tartan skirt. Her name and the address where she was currently living were inked in the most beautiful handwriting, quite possibly even calligraphy. The person in America whom she had contacted via the

Dark Web, who went by the username *Mephistopheles76*, obviously had some talent.

After nervously playing with her long red locks for a while, the woman decided she was being silly, and it was time to open the letter. She reckoned she was being daft for even being interested in the Dark Arts at all, as many had told her over the years, including Peter. "A load of old horse shit, the biggest lot of mumbo jumbo ever, nonsense old wives' tales," he would tell her with a scorning mockery. She couldn't help it, though. The real world was boring and tedious at the best of times. It was just a bit of harmless fun, a little bit of intrigue, and an interest she had obviously inherited from her mother and her mother before her.

Suddenly, she lifted the letter in both hands and violently ripped off the white paper envelope, revealing its contents.

It was an old black-and-white photograph.

The picture had weathered over the years and looked somewhat faded, with a crease at the top right-hand corner. It featured some small black children, boys and girls, all preteens, probably aged around ten years or less. They were standing together in a meadow of sorts, facing the camera with their arms linked. None of them were smiling, all looking rather gravely towards the camera. The girl in the centre was wearing an extremely unsettling, malevolent-looking demonic mask. Below the picture, written crudely on its edge, was the following:

The Children of Chax, Republic of Haiti, 1932.

The woman studied the picture for around a minute. *This is indeed all so very silly*, she ruminated. *Peter will make fun of me if he finds out, and he will be just right, too, especially when he notices that his bank account is a little lighter this month after I paid five hundred pounds of his hard-earned cash to obtain this apparently very rare and cursed image. It's all pretty ridiculous, like he says, sitting alone in an empty house on the Shankill and staring at an old photo. Probably another foolish victim of an Internet scam!*

She stared in silence at the photograph for another couple of minutes before deciding it was time to leave and get back into her car, putting all this nonsense behind her and making the drive back to County Armagh. She reckoned she could maybe hit the gym for an hour or two to help release all this nervous tension inside of her.

As she stood up and went to slip the photo into her blouse pocket, she jumped back after noticing, or at the very least thinking she noticed, something out of the corner of her eye. She could have sworn the image on the picture moved a little.

She quickly put the photo up to the front of her face and studied it in detail, her eyes narrowing as she focused on it. What she saw made her heart sink, causing her to grab for the wooden chair, fumbling a little for it and then sitting back down again, not once blinking or taking her eyes off the image. She reckoned it was probably just her imagination, or some sort of optical illusion, a trick of the light, but she was almost certain the little girl in the demonic mask had moved forward a few steps.

Yes, she definitely did! All those kids were in a straight line before, but now she has moved forward a little! This is really weird. The woman blinked.

Intensely, she zoned in on the photograph for a few minutes, noting every single detail. Focusing, focusing, focusing.

And then it happened. The children in the photograph began to move. Slightly at first, but then casually in front of the woman's very eyes, in almost three dimensions, all the children, in their torn, ragged clothing, moved forward a few strides and then formed a circle, arms linked once again. The young Caribbean kids then moved anti-clockwise in the circle, before the masked girl broke from the chain and into the centre. There she danced a strange dance, contorting her body in impossible ways, whilst the other youngsters chanted an incantation—some sort of dark prayer perhaps, something unholy for sure—in a rhythmic, repetitive, unnatural tone.

The woman dropped the photograph onto the floor in a panicked haste and buried her face in her hands, rubbing her eyes, both horrified and astonished at the same time. When she eventually removed her hands and opened her eyes again, she stared down at the picture on the ground.

It was just as it was when she first witnessed it. Not moving. Back to normal. Still and silent.

What the fuck is going on here? This can't be real. This must be some sort of magic trick or prank. Or maybe I'm having an acid flashback or such from my days as a partygoer. No way can this be real!

She stared at the photograph and then into space for quite some time.

Then a window inside her mind opened and strange voices began talking incessantly inside her head.

Timid, quiet, slow at first:

Hello, can you hear me?

Where are you?

Where am I?

I can't see.

It's dark down here, so very dark.

Are you here? I've been having bad dreams again, my dear.

Most of the voices were female, desperate sounding. Some of them were male, but they were mostly unintelligible and very difficult to understand. The female voices were familiar, but became distant, before suddenly increasing in tone and volume again.

We are in the dark place now, the never-ending region of everlasting pain.

Humiliation all around us.

Save us, please!

We are the damned ones.

Can you hear us?

Swiftly, there were loud screams from the voices before returning to the chattering again, but this time in sentences of gibberish, nonsensical words, almost as if they were speaking backwards. Then the voices turned extremely nasty, cursing and verbally abusing the woman with taunts of a sexual nature—*Whore! Cocksucker! Bastard slut-child Jezebel!*

The woman could now hear her grandmother's voice in there cursing her, too. The voices and background screams increased in noise level again, speaking faster and faster, louder and louder, reaching an unbearable level. The woman stood up quickly and put her hands on her head, shaking it violently whilst crying and screaming and begging the voices to stop, but they refused to relent, becoming more and more intensified. Then a very well-known voice spoke loudly over the rest of the tormenting cries.

It was that of her dead best friend, Laura, and she was screeching.

You fucking bitch. I hate you! You bought those drugs on that night I died. The ones that fucking killed me! I didn't want to take them, but you made me. You put the pressure on me. You promised me it would be fun. You swore that no harm would come to us. But it did—well, to me, anyway. I hate you. You fucking murdered me!

The woman screamed out, "I'm sorry, Laura! I'm so, so sorry!"

The other voices reached a fever pitch, screaming and cursing and insulting and bellowing inside of the woman's head, more and more, angrier and angrier, until some sort of switch inside her mind flicked and she lost her sanity completely, dropping to the floor beside the old black and white photograph, soon slipping out of consciousness.

The last thing she saw before fading away into darkness was the photo beside her, a new image now engrained on it, at the front of the line of young Haitian children. It was a face. A face not of this world, one of pure maliciousness, of depravity and Satanic intent. The face was a combination of the woman's own face and that of the mask the little girl in the picture was wearing. An image that in itself could send even the very strongest of minds into the depths of despair.

Peter drove straight to the mental health facility as soon as the police had contacted him about the incident with his wife in the derelict house on the Shankill. They had been alerted by one of the mothers of some local boys who had heard screaming and broke into the house to find the woman face down on the floor, collapsed and out cold. They tracked Peter down through the personalised number plate on the sports car in front of the house that she had arrived in.

The doctor at the hospital allowed Peter to visit his wife in the room where she was being monitored and kept for her own safety. She was conscious but unresponsive, her face frozen in a look of abject terror, eyes wide open and unblinking.

When the woman's desperately concerned husband enquired as to what had happened to her, he was met with shrugs and shakes of the head. Although examinations of her were apparently ongoing, her preliminary diagnosis was that she had fallen victim to some extreme, sudden shock.

As Peter left the hospital to alert relatives of the situation, he was called back by one of the male psychiatric nurses who had forgotten to give him his wife's possessions, those items found on her at the time she was discovered: a packet of cigarettes, a lighter, a set of keys, an iPhone, and an old, crumpled photograph. Peter put the belongings into his pocket and glanced at the photo of the small black children in the meadow. He thought it odd that his wife would have such an item in her possession and couldn't quite understand it at all.

After placing the photo into the inside pocket of the jacket of his designer suit, he got into his car and decided he would head straight home and study this strange picture some more.

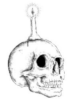

HARVEST

That was black magic, and it was easy to use.
Easy and fun. Like Legos.
- Jim Butcher

The masked entity prepared its unholy altar. A creature of darkness who once took human form seemingly aeons ago, if measured in the trivial terms that mankind attests to in his vain and limited scope.

Very little is known of this timeless being, although in rare whispered, knowing circles, it is reckoned that as a man some centuries ago, he once falsely incriminated a certain well-thought-of carpenter for the toll of a measly bag of silver coins. Before this, and after, the entity had been and would be known by many other titles—Baal, Titivillus, Azazal, Beliar, and Herne the Hunter being just some of the many designations presented to this prince of the underworld.

The altar was in a mostly unknown cave, deep under a picturesque hilly area in the city of Belfast in twenty-first century Northern Ireland. A land that was humble at times, but one cursed and soaked with the blood of its ancestors—combatants and fools in a protracted tribal war between two related sects, fighting against their neighbours in the name of the same Judeo-Christian God. Lucifer himself must have really chuckled at that one. The lives of the innocent suffered the most at the hands of evil men.

A circle of salt was formed around the altar. Black candles were lit on the long, rotting, wooden table in the dripping, cold chamber, surrounded by the cunning being's grimoire of incantations, ancient crystals, reverse talismans, and a ceremonial blade. Many insects of the earth, such as beetles, woodlouse, millipedes, and spiders scuttled over and around the wood. The entity—let's call it a Soul Devourer—was covered in its liturgical deep red robes and cloak, and had with it a cumbersome sack, one which moved and jerked oddly, making strange inhuman screeching sounds at the same time.

The contents of the sack—a domestic tomcat, a Jack Russell terrier, a cockerel, and a bird of the air, a crow—were emptied forthwith onto the decrepit, death-smelling table. Fighting and clawing at each other in sheer panic and desperation, the poor animals were covered in bloodied scrapes and gashes resulting from their blind fight with each other for survival. One of the front legs of the cat had almost been ripped from its body, hanging on by a tendril, while the dog's left eye was now removed from the socket, a reddened, soaking hole in its place. The rumpled crow was dazed and confused, as the cockerel stumbled while trying to walk on broken limbs. Hair and feathers filled the air, as dark bodily fluids from the four beasts soaked the altar, all the while as they clawed and pecked in disorientated desperation; the scene would be almost comic if the circumstances were not so gravely depraved.

The Soul Devourer calmly and routinely clutched each dumb, although generally harmless, living organism in turn by the neck and removed each of their heads swiftly with the razor-sharp ceremonial dagger, lopping them towards the centre of the makeshift altar whilst dropping the torsos on the ground at first, before picking them up at the end of the slaughter and setting them beside the rest of the remains on the table. As it lay on the putrid altar of sin, the decapitated body of the cockerel twitched due to its now failing internal neural networks.

After the macabre sacrifice to its immediate superiors and ultimate Master, the Soul Devourer turned its attention to the grimoire and the recitation of some of the rites contained within, inked in what is believed by some to be human blood. The diabolical chant performed was not of this celestial sphere and indeed belonged only to a ghastly and terrible region of another dimension altogether—that of the fiery lake of burning sulphur and the second death, wherein beholds a never-ceasing wailing and gnashing of teeth.

At the completion of the ritual, the strange figure extinguished the black candles and made haste for the exit of the cave and into the surrounding misty early morning woods ahead, making tracks to the area where its superiors had just revealed would contain its long-craved-after reward—a nourishing feast indeed, and a human sacrifice to be offered up with glee.

The Cruel and Forbidden Ones would be most pleased.

Mark enjoyed jogging a lot. It helped clear his head and essentially keep him sane. There was a lot of stigma still attached to mental illness in Northern Ireland, so there was no way in the world that he was ever going to admit to Joe Public that he had recently been diagnosed with bipolar disorder. Not a chance of it, he reckoned. And that's if he was even really mentally ill in the first place, as that condescending psychiatrist had concluded. They love to put labels on people, stick them in a box and throw a load of happy pills down their gullets until they don't know what day it is, or what planet they're on. Control, that's what it's all about, mused Mark, as he stepped up his pace on the Upper Crumlin Road and onto the Horse Shoe Bend.

Mark hadn't taken his medication in weeks and, if truth be told, he was still arrogantly in denial of Dr. Rainey's medical opinion of what he suffered from. On a generous day he would perhaps offer up the suggestion that what he really suffered from was in fact *drug-induced* bipolar, as the delusions and deep depression quite often followed an intense weed-smoking session. He didn't smoke quite as much now anyway, certainly nowhere near as much as he would have in his teenage years and twenties, which was basically all day, every day. But now at thirty-two years of age he felt he no longer needed it as much and had somewhat grown out of the phase. Those couple of enforced stays at Knockbracken Mental Health Facility had certainly given him food for thought regarding his lifestyle, too. That, and a few nervous breakdowns.

Deep down, however, in some remote back corner of his very essence, Mark knew rightly that he wasn't well, and the medical professionals were right. He just simply could not admit it. But running at the crack of dawn—when all was serene and most mere mortals were still enjoying the slumber of the hard-worked and downtrodden—was the time Mark enjoyed most. When he could almost touch and feel his peace of mind, and where his manic racing brain could be tamed for a little while.

The Cavehill area of North Belfast has, in recent times, been rather popular with outdoorsy sporting types—hikers, cyclists, dog walkers (if that can be considered a sport), those ridiculous-looking power walkers who move like they've soiled themselves, and, of course, the joggers like Mark Tate. Oh, and let us also not forget the teenage drinkers who congregate in the region on the weekends, their rave music pumping obnoxiously loud for all and sundry nearby to be deafened by.

The region itself could be best described as a wooded hill that the locals have always claimed to be a mountain. But it's not a mountain; it's a big hill at best. The peak of the summit is the rocky "Napoleon's Nose," a cliff of sorts that is host to, it must be said, the most splendid view imaginable, which takes in most of East Belfast, Belfast Harbour, Newtownabbey, and to the right, Newcastle, County Down and the Mountains of Mourne sweeping down to the sea. On a really good day, you can even see Scotland across the lough, and to the direct left of Napoleon's Nose is Belfast Zoo with all its lions and tigers and bears, oh my. On the cliff face are a couple of caves, and the foot of the cliff leads into more woodland, eventually running down to the grounds of the Belfast Castle, built in the nineteenth century. The whole area is truly beauteous and awe-inspiring and certainly one of the jewels in Belfast's oft-troubled crown.

Rumours had always abounded, though, of the general terrain being historically host to druid activity and even that of the Dark Arts. The great scenery, however, was one of the other main reasons that Mark enjoyed running there.

It was a particularly mild early spring morning, with the dew moistening most of the surroundings, and Mark's breath was visible as he huffed and puffed his way onto the Hightown Road and towards the side entrance to the now council-run Cavehill Country Park. It was shortly after seven-thirty, so the place was still very much unpopulated, something which suited the runner perfectly.

Mark, who could certainly feel himself getting fitter and healthier with these morning exercises, rounded the entrance to Cavehill Country Park, breezed past the carpark and the picnic tables and on down the pathway that would eventually lead him to the main hill and wooded areas. The cows in the fields beside the dirt track where he moved watched him with a vague, casual disinterest, obviously now well used to the sight of human life in all its ridiculous forms entering their domain. A few rays of sunlight were trying to creep through the morning mist like inter-dimensional alien burglars trying to break into our universe.

The dusty path led downhill slightly, eventually taking Mark to the usual crossroads he had approached many mornings before. He had the choice of going left and up the Cavehill, which would soon take him to the top, the wondrous view, and onto Napoleon's Nose, or take the right path, which would take him around the side of the mountain, past the quarry where a woman's body was found strangled and beaten some years prior, through some woodland and eventually onto the grounds of Belfast Castle.

After a couple of minutes' pause, mainly to catch his breath and stretch a bit, he decided upon taking the right-hand path, the reason being that the upward stretch to the top of the Cavehill was a tough one on the legs, feeling almost vertical at certain points. It wasn't much of a day to enjoy the view up there with the mist making it difficult to fully appreciate, but he fancied the change from his usual route anyway. Once he reached the castle grounds, he could jog on down to the Antrim Road, take a right onto the North Circular Road, leading on to the Ballysillan Road, and then home for a shower and some breakfast.

It was a decision he would soon regret in the gravest of manners.

The wild horses in the field beside the country track Mark was now pacing on were playing and galloping away idly, beautiful creatures enjoying the morning and the full splendour of the natural world at its finest. They barely even noticed the jogger as he passed by them, but when he spied them with their frivolous, innocent nature it brought a smile to his face.

An early-rising dog-walker was the only other human being Mark saw that day as he paced past the old quarry at the side of the main hill; he greeted the elderly man with the usual pleasantries, which were returned.

As the wooded region approached, the thirty-two-year-old stopped to catch his breath again. He was thirsty and was now regretting not bringing a bottle of water with him on his journey. He had no choice but to press on regardless, into the trees and forest which awaited him with a gaping mouth.

Birds chirped a pleasant song overhead whilst the surrounding trees and growth seemed to ooze with a living vibrancy. The spirit of the surrounding nature was filled with vitality. Mark felt good. He felt truly alive, at one with his environment and immersed in the feeling that he was living life the way it was truly intended.

As he rounded a sharp bend on the dirt road he was treading on, Mark glimpsed something out of the corner of his left eye that he had never noticed before. Although he usually took the other route on the Cavehill during his morning runs, he knew the general area pretty well and had quite a few times taken the same path he was on now. Through the trees and overgrowth on his left side was a rather odd sight and one that gave him a feeling of deep disorientation. There was a house, a single-floored cottage, apparently derelict for some time. A dirty-looking place, perhaps a couple of hundred years old at least. Surely, he could not have missed seeing this all the times he had been past the exact same area before, Mark thought, while at the same time filled with both curiosity and unease. The outside walls of the house were stone and had at one point in their past been painted white, but the paint had now greatly faded. There were two glassless windows with black curtains draped on the inside, an ancient-looking oak door at the front, a smoking chimney on top, and all around and over it was a mass of twisted moss and weeds.

The surrounding area was now in complete silence. A stunned, unnatural silence. The air had turned chilly, suddenly much colder than just before, and upon impulsively checking his wristwatch Mark found to his confusion that the minutes and seconds hands were rotating backwards of their own accord, anti-clockwise. He felt nauseous and suspected he was becoming sick again. He had been doing great of late but now felt like he was on the onset of another bipolar episode and maybe even a full breakdown. He contemplated that he could be suffering from some delusions again, whilst attempting to compose and steady his being through the controlled breathing exercises he had been taught at the "nervous" hospital.

Sick or not, the house still seemed very real in his mind and was a conundrum Mark wanted to get to the bottom of, at the very least to put the mystery in his mind to rest and feed his increasing nervous inquisitiveness. He put his hands briefly over his face, rustled his blond hair, and decided to walk towards the mysterious house.

The damp oak door was slightly ajar, and Mark now noticed some etchings on the front of it—scrawlings carved in a peculiar language unbeknownst to him. A verse it seemed, a poem perhaps. A solitary black crow sat on the roof above the door in silence, its deviously dark eyes watching his every move, almost motionless, yet its glare almost piercing right through his body. The bird's eyes followed his every step as he opened the door and entered the hallway, while a feeling of impending doom rushed over his body. As Mark stepped into the house, a putrid stench of decaying death filtered into his nostrils, almost overcoming him.

The walls in the hallway were filthy, smeared in excrement and dirt. The floor was covered in dead leaves and other debris, such as the carcasses of birds and rodents, their bloodied and mashed-up innards being gorged on hurriedly by insect life, scurrying and fighting with each other for the tastiest, most nourishing parts. It was almost as if this rancid place was home to *anti*-nature, with death and negativity all around.

In front of Mark there were doorless entrances to four rooms, two on each side. He walked into the first one on the left, now in some sort of trance of trepidation.

More of the same vile mess and corpses of birds and cats littered the ground, but on the crumbling, once white wall facing the door-way, there was a message scribed in huge, messily written words. It appeared they'd had been authored in blood.

O HUMAN RACE, BORN TO FLY UPWARD,
WHEREFORE AT A LITTLE WIND DOST THOU SO FALL?

Below the writings was the image of an upside-down cross with a crudely drawn serpent wrapped around it, also daubed in blood. Bloodied human handprints were also imprinted on the walls of this horrid room, with Mark noticing that blood seemed to be dripping from the right-hand curtain at the window. He went over to investigate more, transfixed with the horror show in front of him.

The jet-black, thick, silken drapes had more of the strange in-decipherable letterings and symbols on them. Mark had never seen this form of language or written word before, but somehow, he could sense that there was something very old and unholy con-cerning everything about this wicked place. Was he sick and hav-ing some sort of awful hallucination—perhaps lying somewhere on the Cavehill, unconscious and dreaming a nightmare of intense horrors? He simply couldn't tell anymore but decided upon exiting this room to investigate the rest of the squalid surroundings.

Two of the other three rooms were quite similar to the first one he had witnessed—rotting death and sacrilegious graffiti—but the far room to the right, the last one Mark entered, was something altogether different. It was warm and almost welcoming. There was a lit open fire at the centre of the far wall, the source of the smoke coming from the chimney outdoors. The flames crackled and danced from the wood excitedly, like little fire sprites or imps, and they seemed to be emitting a strange, though pleasant-smelling, perfume-like odour, too. The ceiling and walls were covered in the most beautiful if somewhat macabre and vivid artwork, covering almost the entirety of them and depicting graphic scenes from epic battles between the forces of light and darkness. Demons, abominations, some winged and airborne, with features resembling the likes of frogs, many-headed dragons, snakes, and other devils, were torturing and slaying apparent angels, decapitating them, impaling them, violating them. Some of the devils were horned and others even had faces on their backsides.

In the centre of the room was an altar, a table covered in the same silken, black, symbol-laden material that was used for the curtains in the other rooms. On the altar were two human skulls circled by ignited black candles, and in the centre was a large, very sharp, exquisite dagger.

Mark was dazed by everything in front of his eyes—enchanted even—with the aroma of the sweet-smelling fumes from the fire filling his nose, lungs, and head, dizzying him greatly. He tried to fight it at first but with no success, as the scent and fumes only got stronger and stronger until he could barely see in front of him.

The last thing Mark saw before collapsing was a huge dark green snake darting at him from under the altar table and biting him on the right ankle. Then everything in his head faded to complete darkness...

When Mark regained consciousness, he awoke in the same room. Everything was the same as it had been before, but the snake was nowhere to be seen. He had no idea how long he had been passed out. His throat was dry, and he stumbled as he tried to stand up. The weird though pleasant aroma was even stronger in the room now. It seemed to somewhat ease and calm him. He was now feeling a little outside of himself, his senses fully heightened, fully aware of everything around him and in the room. It felt good, almost sexual, even.

He believed he could see strange, irregular shapes jumping out at him from the darkness, shapes with faces intent on malevolence, but for some reason he was no longer afraid. He welcomed them, in fact, and laughed maniacally to himself. These alien sensations, feelings and visions grew and grew, until reaching a fever pitch so intense Mark thought he might explode.

He lost his mind completely around this point, his sanity slipping away like a fish escaping a net.

The frenzied and hypnotised Mark Tate walked calmly to the Satanic altar and lifted the ceremonial dagger in his best hand, the right one. He tilted his head back slowly, exposing his raw throat, and raised the blade before slamming it into his trachea, playing around inside of it for a short while before collapsing on the floor once again, deep crimson spurting and flowing from his gaping wound.

As he lay on the ground with his life force ebbing rapidly away, Mark's thoughts turned briefly to the pleasant sight of the horses he had seen playing in the field earlier, and then finally to terror and deep regret. Then it was all over for him in this world.

The Soul Devourer arrived at the house soon after to claim its reward from the Cruel and Forbidden Ones. It was still dressed elegantly in its red ceremonial robes and cloak, with its goat's head mask covering its diabolical, otherworldly facial features. Its immediate superiors had once again laid a trap for an unsuspecting member of the human race, who had fallen for it hook, line and sinker. The deception was now complete, and the fresh soul was ready for harvesting by the cloaked entity standing in front of the now lifeless body.

Mark Tate's soul would soon be feasted upon and then dragged to the nethermost depths of eternal darkness and never-ending torment.

His second death was imminent.

LIGHTNING IN A BOTTLE

*S*o I was completely fucking pished out of my head, lying slumped in the corner of my desolate, debris-laden one-room bedsit on Belfast's Shore Road.

I was unshaven with my hair totally unkempt, so greasy and dirty you could easily have believed I had just stuck my head in a chip pan. Actually, now that I mention it, at that precise moment in time, I would have happily stuck my head in an oven, never mind a chip pan. But I digress; so back to the story at hand.

I was on the floor caressing my now empty cider bottle, the contents of which I had just greedily guzzled. As I continued to stroke its green glass in an almost sexual manner whilst wearing nothing but my pish-stained *A-Team* boxer shorts, a rather strange occurrence proceeded to unfold in front of my highly intoxicated eyes.

A misty blue smoke suddenly rose from inside the bottle, slowly filling the room around me. In my infinite wisdom, I immediately thought to myself, *Ahh fuck, not another bout of the DTs!* but I may very well have been mistaken this time as I hadn't had a vision as intense as this one in quite some time. This was more the sort of shit I would have seen during those more halcyon 1990s rave days of Speckled Doves, Micro Dots, and Purple Ohms.

Anyway, the strange blue smoke was swirling in odd motions and irregular directions whilst tentacled monstrous beings and quaint dragons began to form in its midst. It all felt like I had just landed unannounced into the middle of a fucking H.P. Lovecraft story, or accidentally wandered onto the set of an episode of *The*

Twilight Zone, such was the vividness of what was appearing before me.

But as quickly as the mysterious blue smoke had appeared, it soon vanished again, leaving in its place the most beautiful woman I have ever laid eyes upon in my entire life. She was clothed in a majestic satin purple dress, her jet-black hair tied back in a pony-tail, her shapely breasts only adding to the overall effect. She reminded me of the sort of exotic princess you would have seen in those old Sinbad films, the ones with the really cool Ray Harry-hausen stop-motion special effects.

I asked the fair damsel who the fuck she was and how she managed to get into my humble abode, but then I remembered that I'd probably left the front door lying wide open because I was drunk as fuck and always did extremely stupid shit like that when I was, like the time I stole the kid's bike and pedalled off into the sunset—I mean towards the off-license—but ended up crashing into a wall and breaking my arm. I'm digressing again.

The mesmerizing lady who had appeared from out of nowhere replied to me in a sultry Middle Eastern accent that she was in fact a genie whom I had just summoned. She told me she could grant me three wishes which would undoubtedly come true the instant I made them.

Of course, I was at first a little bit incredulous to her wild claims but then, almost instinctively, I had a "fuck it, why not?" moment and decided to play along with the young woman's game.

As I had just run out of my precious apple-based beverage, my obvious first choice was for an endless supply of more of the same. The moment my mouth spoke the words, my bedsit was suddenly filled with a seemingly never-ending supply of "barrack busters" of Ye Olde English Medium Dry Cyder variety. It was a miracle! It was almost like I had died and undeservedly gone to Heaven.

The genie then told me I had two wishes left, so after taking a large swig from one of my newly acquired bumper bottles of the sweet-tasting bevvy, I pondered for a little while, not wanting to make any rash decisions.

Eventually, and because I was a lonely bastard and still am, I asked the magical woman politely for some female companionship. In my typical sly way, I was secretly hoping in a less than subtle manner that she would take me up on my irresistible offer herself and be up for a bit of a roll around, but alas she did not appear to be in the slightest bit interested, and I can't say I fucking blamed her as I was in a right royal mess.

Instead, the "lady" of my dreams did indeed arrive in a puff of blue smoke in the form of a Rough Collie dog, barking and yelping excitedly in my face like Lassie on amphetamines.

Now, I like dogs and all sorts of other animals, but not in that way. I'm not like one of those weird bastards you often see on obscure late-night documentaries on Channel 4 or *The Jeremy Kyle Show*, so I simply got up and offered my new-found canine friend a treat in the form of an out-of-date Kit Kat, to which it promptly declined, probably wisely.

My dazzling genie visitor then reminded me that I had just the one wish left.

I thought long and hard, more than I had ever done in my life before.

After quite some time, I eventually reached my moment of true enlightened clarity. An epiphany.

You know, I may have behaved like a right cunt for a large section of my life, but it was now time to set the record straight, put the past behind me, and do something truly, properly good for a change.

So, I wished for world peace.

"It is done!" exclaimed the genie before dissolving for good in a haze of blue smoke. Naturally.

I was simply overjoyed at what I had achieved during this freaky night in my lowly little flat. I really felt I had finally made a huge difference to this planet for the greater good once and for all!

I decided to celebrate my euphoric, deeply satisfying happiness with a nice big glass of cold cider. And another one. And another. And another. And another...

I woke up abruptly on the floor again early the next morning to the sight of my new pet—which incidentally I have now named Benji—licking my face. The countless cider bottles were still lying everywhere around my main living area, quite a few of them now empty, too. It looked like I hadn't dreamt all that crazy nonsense after all, and that knowledge gave me a warm feeling within of great hope.

Remarkably, I didn't even have a hangover either. I felt fresh, fit, and healthy, looking forward to the day ahead and what pleasures it had in store for me. My insatiable yearning for the demon drink had also apparently left my being, and that was a relief words themselves could not express.

I sprang up with a smug smile pasted upon my face and made my way to the front door of my bedsit and into the sunshine that awaited me outside.

As I walked out into the glorious day ahead, my mood quickly changed from one of jubilation to one of confusion, and then to sheer horror and realisation.

Bodies lay motionless everywhere. On the footpaths. On the roads. At the bus stops. In the crashed cars. There were no real injuries on anyone either. No blood and guts. It was as if everyone had just stopped breathing together, all at the very same time. The atmosphere of complete silence was deafening in its eeriness. It appeared I was now the last man on Earth, like some sort of shite version of Charlton Heston in *The Omega Man*.

Ah well, I thought to myself, *at least I still have my cider*.

CHARGING THE LIGHT BRIGADE

Stop a foot and cast an eye,
As you are now so once was I.
As I am now so you will be,
Prepare for death and follow me.
- Inscription on a gravestone, Shankill Graveyard, Belfast

Despite it being Christmas Eve, twelve-year-old Billy Bickerstaff had never felt so depressed in his entire life. Life at home was crap. Really crap. And at school, it was even worse. He missed his old primary school. Life was so much better then. Year 8 at the Boys Model was the worst ever, thanks to Kyle Weir and his mates who were making his life hell. The bullying messages and comments on Facebook and Instagram were one thing, but did they really have to flush his head down that *used* toilet last month, making him the laughingstock of the entire school and beyond, and was not exactly helpful when he burst out crying afterwards in front of them all? He hated that fat asshole Kyle, and the older boys in general, and would do anything to get his own back on him, but alas he just wasn't brave or tough enough to go through with it. Maybe one day he would when he was bigger, then they'd pay for ruining his life. Billy supposed he could have gotten him back by reporting him to the teachers, but that would have just made things worse for him. *Much* worse.

He could hear their usual taunts ringing in his head constantly: *Little cry-baby. Billy the loser, the little mummy's boy who couldn't fight to save his life.* Those sorts of things. But the stuff about his granda was the lowest point. His granda's recent death had really affected him badly; the man had taught him how to swim and so much more. They were very close and did so much together. Right up until that day on the previous January when his granda went outside on a sunny Saturday morning to change the tyre on his car only to suffer a massive heart attack, dead before he hit the ground, right in front of the shocked eyes of several other of the residents of Silverstream Drive where he lived. Those bullies had no right whatsoever to make fun of Billy about this.

His older sister Caroline wasn't much help to him either these days, and quite the little madam at times, too. They used to get on really well when they were smaller, but now she was more into boys and going out clubbing on the weekends with her friends. She no longer had the time to go to the cinema or hang out with Billy. He had very few friends anyway, and he just wished things could go back to the way they were between them, joking around and laughing like they used to. Now she was just a miserable, moody cow who dressed and acted like a vampire with her weirdo Goth clothes, makeup, and music.

As he mulled over his troubles from the sanctity of his bedroom, Billy decided to himself that he really needed to make more of an effort with his life once Christmas and the New Year period was over. He was tired of moping around, locking himself away and being a soft touch. In the new year, he was going to change for the better. He would get out more, make new friends, maybe even get a girlfriend for the very first time, stand up for himself and no longer be a walkover. He was sick of spending his free time stuck at home.

He wasn't even looking forward to Christmas as much as he used to. The magic of it had left him. He wanted to change though, for things to be like they were before again, but it all seemed like too much effort. It was so hard for him to get motivated to do anything lately.

Eventually, he decided to go downstairs and watch a bit of Christmas TV with his mother. At least it would be a slight change of scenery from the four walls of his bedroom, still adorned with posters of pop stars he didn't even like anymore. It would be some company for both of them, before his da arrived home later.

He slumped down the stairs and into the living room where he sat on the sofa beside the Christmas tree with her. She was watching an old black and white film about a slim, yet handsome and troubled man named George Bailey. *It's a Wonderful Life*, it was called. A wonderful life indeed.

As the film was ending with the suicidal George Bailey realising the error of his ways and deciding to spend Christmas with his wife and children after all, while the supporting cast sang "Hark! The Herald Angels Sing" and an annoying little girl delivered a line about angels getting their wings every time a bell rings, there was suddenly a large crash at Billy's front door. His father had arrived home early, even more drunk than usual, it appeared. As he stumbled into the living room, Billy noticed that his father had that intense drunken stare about his countenance again, the wild, insane-looking eyes. He didn't always have that look about him when he drank, but when he did, Billy knew it meant only one thing: there would be violence and screaming. And lots of it.

The arguing came first, as it always did, the volume of the voices rising with each volatile sentence. Then came the excessive punches raining down on Billy's mother's head. The lunging kicks next. Then the loud screams and swearing. Billy couldn't take it anymore. He had seen it happen so many times before, and he was no match physically for his six-foot father to do anything. He obeyed what his instincts told him to do, despite how cowardly it made him feel, and made a run for it, straight out the front door and into the cold, dark night ahead of him.

A translucent moon hung in the heavens above, as Billy hurriedly made his way down his terraced street. He passed warm, cosy-looking houses adorned with Christmas decorations, the occupants of their brightly shining living rooms huddled around flat-screen televisions with children playing games on their phones and iPads. When he arrived at the top of the street, he turned a sharp left onto the main Shankill Road and began walking quickly in the direction of Woodvale Park. That's where he'd go, he reckoned in his panicked mind. But it was so very cold. During the commotion at his house, he'd fled without his coat and now here he was, properly running away from home for good this time with only his jumper on to keep him warm. Shit one, but he trundled on up the road anyway. At least it wasn't raining or snowing, he thought to himself, as an icy mist seemed to be gradually blanketing the area all around.

It was just after ten p.m., so the main road was still quite well populated, mainly with drunken revellers making their way home as they exited the bars, nearby Chinese takeaway restaurants, and kebab shops. Billy soon passed the Northern Ireland Supporters' Club, Shakin' Stevens' "Merry Christmas Everyone" blasting from inside somewhere while happy customers sang along and some youths smoked at the front of the building.

He crossed the road at Lanark Way and onto the beginning of the adjoining Woodvale Road, just opposite the Shankill Graveyard, when he noticed three women, possibly in their late forties, approaching him. They were very drunk, wearing clothing not exactly in keeping with the current weather; short skirts and tops revealing their more than ample cleavages. One of them, the apparent leader, was a blonde woman with a comedic Santa hat fitted misshapenly on her head. The other two had tinsel wrapped around their necks. Billy hoped upon hope that they wouldn't notice him, as he tried to silently slip by them undetected and without making eye contact, but it was not to be as the blonde woman clocked him almost straight away and spoke up.

"Awk, girls. Look at this poor wee lad here, out on his own on a cold night like this. What's the matter with you, son? You look upset, and what are you doing without a coat in this freezing cold?"

"I... I left it in the house. I don't need it. I'm just going for a walk and want to be left alone, okay?" stuttered the embarrassed Billy.

"What do you mean you're just going for a walk? On a night like this? What's the matter, son, has someone annoyed you or something?" replied Blondie.

"I've just been having a really bad day and need to get away from everyone and everything. I don't really wanna talk about it, thanks."

The three women stared at him in drunken pity and confusion, not really knowing what to properly do or say. Blondie spoke again. "Aww, ya poor wee lamb, ya. Look, it's Christmas Eve. You should be in your warm bed right now all excited for Santa arriving with loads of presents for you."

"I'm not a kid. It's not like I still believe in Santa. Just leave me alone!" stated Billy abruptly.

"Awk, I know you're not a kid. Look, my name's Andrea and these are my friends, Lizzie and Sally. We're just heading home after a Christmas party. C'mon and we'll walk you home and get you back safely to your wee mummy."

"No! I don't want to go home—not tonight or ever again!"

The brown-haired Lizzie approached Billy next and embraced him, hugging him tightly and kissing him on the cheek, her boobs almost falling out of her low-cut top. "Awk, now. Don't be like that, son. I'm sure your mummy is worried sick about ya. C'mon, take my hand and we'll walk you home."

Billy felt both angry and awkward at the same time, as he tried to break free from Lizzie's grip. He just wished these mad drunken women would piss off and leave him alone once and for all.

He eventually squirmed free from her and bolted across the main road, narrowly avoiding being run over by several cars. A passing driver with ALPHA TAXIS emblazoned on the roof of his car swore out of his side window at him and gave him the middle finger, while the three well-meaning women stood on the other side of the road with their mouths wide open, not wanting to give chase in their high heels. Billy was too fast for them anyway. He wanted to get offside as quickly as his feet would carry him, but Woodvale Park was too far up the road now, so the nearest decent hiding place would have to do.

That came in the form of the Shankill Graveyard, the front gates of which he was now at. But the gates were padlocked shut, so Billy had no other option but to scale the wall and railings beside them, which he did, awkwardly. With his adrenaline pumping, he eventually clambered over the spiked rails, being careful not to impale himself on them, and dropped to the other side and into the deserted old historical cemetery.

Normally, being in such a place in the dark of night would have terrified Billy, but he had so many other real-life worries to take his mind off such things. All the same, his new surroundings were still very intimidating, the old tombs and gravestones lit eerily in the misty moonlight, and with the trees and bushes at each side of the graveyard rustling in the wind almost as if they were whispering to him the long-forgotten secrets of the ancient dead below his feet, or even trying to warn him about something. The large, domineering statue of Queen Victoria in front of the graves seemed even bigger than usual, towering over the boy, seemingly watching his every move with a haughty scorn, like "one" was not best pleased with his intrusion into this sacred corner of her kingdom. Billy tried to put his Gothic surroundings to the back of his mind, as he panted towards one of the nearby benches, his cold, icy breath clearly visible in front of his eyes.

He sat down on a bench and attempted to gather himself together and correlate in his head everything that had just happened to him in such a short space of time. It wasn't easy, though. He was out of breath and beginning to feel the sharp cold again, his emotions running high and feeling thoroughly dejected. He held his head in his hands and pondered how this was indeed the worst Christmas ever and how he could never go home again now.

Billy wept.

Shaking and sobbing uncontrollably, he eventually attempted to compose himself and work out what he should do next. He decided he should stay in the graveyard for a little while more, and then when the main road was quieter, he would sneak up to Woodvale Park where he could head to the glen at the back of the park and try to find somewhere to camp out. It wasn't half bitter though—Baltic, even. He really should have brought his coat with him, but hoped he would indeed find some shelter in the park. He really needed somewhere, and he was becoming more aware of his unsettling vicinity by the minute. The realisation that he was literally surrounded by the bodies of the long dead was beginning to frighten him and play tricks with his mind.

From the side of his eye, almost as quick as a flash, Billy suddenly saw a movement from behind one of the gravestones in front of him. He tried to rationalise it in his young mind by telling himself it was probably just the wind, or older boys out drinking or taking drugs.

Then another movement, followed by a crisp, commanding, well-spoken voice:

"Tally-ho, old chap. I say, what the bloody devil's gotten into you, young fella? What's with all the tears? It looks to me like somebody needs to man up!"

A panic-stricken Billy glanced all around him to see where the odd voice was coming from but couldn't see anyone at all. "Who... who the hell's that? Who's in here with me? Stop trying to scare me. It's not working, you know! Who are ye?"

A moment of tense silence.

Then, as if on command, a tall, strangely dressed figure stepped out from the side of the statue of Queen Victoria, just to the left of where Billy was facing. Despite it being dark and misty, the figure could be clearly seen in the moonlight from above, standing proudly beside the monument of the old monarch. It was a man, dressed in the most bizarre costume, perhaps on his way home from some sort of Christmas fancy dress party, Billy mused. He was wearing a strange type of top hat, a red blazer with white straps on it, and black trousers and boots. The man had obviously been to the fancy dress party as an old-time soldier from some war long ago.

Billy shouted in his direction, "Go away and leave me alone! I'm not in the mood for any jokes tonight. I just want to be left here on my own, in peace. I'm not doing anyone any harm!"

The odd figure responded, "And I certainly don't mean you any harm either, boy. On the contrary, actually. Believe it or not, I'm here to help, young man. May I come over and share a seat with you?"

"You can if you tell me exactly who you are and what you want!"

"Sergeant John Brown of the 17th Lancers cavalry regiment of Her Majesty Queen Victoria's British Army, Charge of the Light Brigade, at your service. And who might you be and why the bloody hell are you dressed so oddly?"

"What... what are you on about? Are you drunk as well, just on your way back from a Christmas party? My name's Billy... Billy Bickerstaff."

The strange man began slowly walking towards the boy.

"Billy Bickerstaff, eh? Not a name I'm familiar with, I can tell you that for nothing. Not a bad name, however. I do like good old manly names like Billy, Charles, Robert, George, and Henry. And nice Biblical names too, you know, Zachariah, Nathaniel, those sorts of ones. No matter, it's a pleasure to make your acquaintance, Billy Bickerstaff. You can call me John, by the way. Now, tell me all about the buggers who have been bothering you, young Bickerstaff."

As the figure approached him, Billy noticed how much of a strikingly tall and handsome man he really was, with his flowing, brownish hair and thick handlebar moustache. He reminded him of the type of person he would often see on TV in one of those Charles Dickens-style costume dramas that he'd glanced at from time to time, usually on a boring Sunday evening when nothing else decent was on. Billy didn't feel threatened by the man, however. Indeed, the man had an extremely calming influence on him, like Billy somehow knew him from somewhere. He felt safe and somewhat protected in his company, the way he used to feel when he was with his granda. Sergeant John Brown soon sat his tightly built frame down beside Billy at the end of the bench.

"Well, move yourself up a bit. You could fit an army on here. C'mon, boy, shift."

Billy did as he was told. "So, who are you, mister? Do I know you from somewhere?"

"I shouldn't bloody well think so, boy. Not unless you're one of my descendants. Let's take a look at those eyes of yours... blue, I see. Nope, definitely not one of mine. Good God in Heaven, I'd love a smoke right now. I do miss my pipe. Unfortunately they didn't bury it with me, the buggers."

"A pipe? You mean like a weed pipe?"

"What the bloody hell's a weed pipe? You mean like a hashish pipe? I once tried a little bit of that back in India—never again, my boy—bloody cloud cuckoo land! No, I mean I miss my old tobacco pipe."

"Why don't you just buy a new one in town or something?"

"My dear boy, things aren't quite as simple as that where I'm from."

"What do you mean? Are you not from round here?"

"No, sadly not. Well, not really, anyway. Not anymore. You might even say I'm completely out of time and place."

"So where are you from then?"

The man paused for a few seconds. "I'm not really too sure, to be honest. I suppose you could say I'm from The Other Side..."

"You mean you're from the Falls?"

"The Falls? I don't think I quite follow you, young Bickerstaff. I was born and raised on the Shankill Road, not far from this graveyard, if you must know. I spent many years away from home, fighting for the Crown in wars long forgotten by most. I don't really come from anywhere now. I died many years ago. I suppose you could say this graveyard is my home now. Well, mine and many others. I do still miss my old mother though, just as much as I did when I was away in all those foreign lands."

John Brown stared ahead of him. Billy was almost certain he could see tears welling up in the man's eyes, but when he noticed the lad was watching him, he quickly composed himself again.

"So, tell me, young Bickerstaff. Who the devil's been bothering you?"

Billy didn't believe in ghosts, but somehow he just knew this man, Sergeant John Brown, was telling him the truth. He didn't feel afraid, though—quite the opposite. He felt an odd connection to him, something he couldn't quite explain or even comprehend. He just knew it felt right.

"I've run away from home, Sergeant Brown."

"And why the blazes would you do something like that then?

And on a freezing cold winter's night like this too! Have you gone stark raving mad, m'boy?"

"I just can't take it anymore."

"Take what? What's the matter with you? C'mon, you can talk to me, Billy."

"I... I... Look, Mr. Brown, it's about my da. I don't really want to talk about it."

"I told you to just call me John. Now come on, young man, spill the beans. What's up with your father?"

A pause.

"It's the drink, John. He drinks too much."

"Likes a tipple then, does he? Like most of us menfolk. So what's the problem?"

"He changes when he's drunk. He gets violent, beats my mummy up. He even threw her down the stairs once and she ended up in hospital. It's like he becomes a different person when he drinks."

"Ah, now I see what you mean. It doesn't take much of a man to beat up a woman, drunk or not. So how come you think running away is going to help anything? Will that not make matters worse?"

"Look, I just can't take it anymore. Everyone hates me, especially those idiots in school."

"I'm sure that's not the case. I know we've only just met but I don't hate you, and I'm sure we can become friends. Who's bothering you in school then?"

"That fat arsehole Kyle Weir and his mates, that's who. Always picking on me, calling me names. They even flushed my head down the toilet one day and now everyone thinks I'm just an idiot that they can push around."

"You need to learn to stand up for yourself, Billy. This Kyle boy, I'm sure he's not as tough as he's making out. If you don't make a stand with him this will continue to happen and only get worse. Do you really want to be the boy that everyone picks on and makes fun of? It's time to man up, old chap!"

"But I can't, I just can't."

"Poppycock! Of course you bloody well can!"

"But... but I'm afraid."

"Of course you are, Billy, but we have to face our fears or else they control us. Being afraid is natural. How do you think I felt during my Crimean days with the enemy fast approaching, all guns blazing and bayonets flashing? Bloody terrifying it was! But courage, real courage, is realising that it's okay to be afraid but doing the right thing anyway, for the greater good."

"I suppose you're right."

"So, are you going to go back home? I think your mother needs you."

"But what about my da? He'll still be there."

"You've got to face him at some point, both of them, actually. Your poor mother will be worried sick about you now."

Billy looked directly into John Brown's eyes. Despite the tough exterior, they were kind eyes.

"I'm really cold. Maybe I should go home. I just don't think I can face my da right now, though."

"But you have to, Billy. Although you might not think it, he probably needs you there as much as your mother does. You have to help them both. It won't be easy, but there's always a way. You've got what it takes, my boy, I know you do."

Billy stood up off the bench and dithered for a few moments.

"Okay then, I'll go back at some point, but not right now. He'll probably fall asleep soon, but in the morning, I'll go home and try to talk to him about his drinking and how it's affecting us all. It'll be Christmas Day anyway, and I don't want to miss getting my presents, either."

"It's Christmas? Good grief! All the more reason to go home now then. On your way then, lad. Skip to it, I don't want to see you back here tonight!"

Billy smiled for the first time in quite a while.

"So who are you, John Brown? Who are you really?"

"Who, me? Oh, it's not important who I am. What is important is that you get home in time for Christmas, boy."

"No, come on. I told you all about my life, so it's only fair that you tell me who exactly you are."

A pause. The sergeant stood up and stared at Billy directly, intensely.

"Stop a foot and cast an eye, as you are now, so once was I. As I am now so you will be, prepare for death and follow me!"

"What? What the heck does that mean?"

Another pause, longer. Eventually the old soldier sat down again and spoke up, this time in a more relaxed tone.

"I was someone once, a very long time ago now. I had a family, just like you. Times were hard but we were happy. Then the war came along, and I had to do my duty for Queen and country. It was only right. Died on the bloody battlefield, I did. At least it was an honourable death, I suppose. I don't really know what I am now, to be honest. A guardian, maybe."

"A guardian?"

"Yes, we're all guardians here, really. The unseen protectors of the Shankill Road. Yes, that's who we are, I think."

"We?"

From seemingly out of nowhere, from behind the gravestones surrounding Billy, another figure appeared, a man. Then another. And another. Then some more, shades of women and children amongst the men, all dressed in old-time clothing, some in mere rags. Billy stood frozen, not quite aghast but mesmerised by the sight of the spectres in front of his very eyes, not fully grasping the spectacle of ever-growing denizens of the graveyard now in the land of the living. The sergeant eventually broke the mood with his officer-class clipped voice.

"I'd like to introduce you to some of my friends and neighbours, young Billy."

A long-haired male figure, dressed in a spectacular buttoned-up red coat and black hat with a feather placed on top of it stepped forward. Sergeant Brown continued: "Billy Bickerstaff, please meet my good friend Corporal William Smith of Captain Coote's Troop. He died on the sixteenth June 1690 on his way to the Boyne, the poor bugger. He was buried here by the very Reverend Rowland Davies, Chaplain to the Williamite Calvary." Corporal William Smith nodded in acknowledgment of Billy. Two more men then moved into view.

"And these fine gents here are the Reverend Isaac Nelson of the Nelson Memorial Church and William 'Bullseye' Braithwaite. The Reverend was once the Nationalist Member of Parliament for County Mayo from 1880 to 1888, and old Bullseye was a crack shot with a rifle and pistol, hence the nickname. He also went on to found the Braithwaite and McCann pub chain in Belfast."

Even more ghosts made themselves visible.

"Meet William S. Baird. He founded the *Belfast Evening Telegraph*. And Sir James Edward Verner here was a Lieutenant Colonel of the East India Company."

A group of several more phantoms was now nearing Billy— women and children. One of them, a woman covered in tattered clothing, made herself known to the startled boy.

"And I'm Margaret Cameron. In 1912, I signed the Ulster Covenant and later went on to serve as a nurse in The Great War. Many of my friends who you now see in front of you also rest here in the mass graves created for them in the 1830s. All victims of cholera and typhoid."

A gobsmacked Billy, his jaw agape, turned to Sergeant John Brown in shocked silence as if he was about to deliver a stream of questions towards him but couldn't quite find the words. Instead, he turned on his heels and ran towards the graveyard railings, panicked, not quite believing what he had just experienced. As he climbed up onto the wall below the railings and lifted his right leg over the steel bars, he turned and looked back into the graveyard.

But it was now empty, devoid of anything living or otherwise. All he could see in front of him was the statue of Queen Victoria, the silent gravestones, the benches and surrounding lawns, bushes, and trees. He quickly turned back and jumped over the railings, landing on the ground with the main Shankill Road below his feet again.

And straight into the path of Kyle Weir and two of his mates.

"Aww, look who it is. Little Billy. the mummy's boy. What's the matter, you wee dickhead? You look like you've had a bit of a fright," said Kyle as his gormless friends giggled moronically in unison.

After everything he had been through tonight, Billy was in no mood whatsoever for Kyle. "None of your business, Kyle. Now piss off and leave me alone."

The statement stunned Kyle. "What did you just say to me, you wee shit? Do you want me to kick you up and down this Shankill Road until you're crying for your mummy again, just like you did in school that day when we flushed your head down the bog, ha ha?"

Billy could feel the anger building up inside him with great gusto. "I said piss off, you fat prick!"

"That's it; you hold him, boys, and I'll beat the crap out of the wee mummy's boy right here and now."

But before Kyle and his two friends could do anything, Billy did something that he had never done before in his entire life. He clenched his fist as hard as he could and aimed a punch in Kyle's direction, smacking him hard on the side of his nose. The bully dropped to the ground, apparently unconscious, blood gushing from both of his nostrils.

Kyle's shocked friends bent over their fallen leader, attempting to resuscitate him. Billy simply turned his back on them and began walking back down the Shankill Road.

As he reached the part of the footpath before the graveyard's end, Billy caught a glimpse of something in the corner of his eye.

He turned around and peered into the cemetery for one last time on what had been a very eventful night indeed.

He was greeted by the sight of a familiar face, one with a very impressive moustache upon it. Sergeant John Brown of the 17th Lancers cavalry regiment of the British Army was standing upright, smiling broadly in Billy's direction, before aiming a proud salute at the boy.

Billy simply grinned, saluted back, and then began the journey home to spend the remainder of Christmas Eve with his mother.

Relating to Thaumaturgy

All that we see or seem, is but a dream within a dream.
- Edgar Allan Poe, "A Dream Within a Dream"

The interior of the factory was familiar, yet unfamiliar. I'd been here before but hadn't. It was neither day, nor night—not even twilight. Sometime altogether different, unique. There were no stars in the sky outside.

Old, friendly faces greeted me. It was great to see my former work colleagues again—it had been too long. But I wasn't here this time to work—I was here for the books.

Those elusive books! The pages of their revered passages had all but eluded me my entire life—damn, I'd even managed to hold them in my hands briefly on several occasions, but they always seemed to slip away. So frustrating!

The books are somewhat related to a small seaside town that contains a lighthouse. That is all I know, and I do not even know how I came by this information—I was never told; I just know it to be true. One day I hope to visit this town, although I suspect it cannot be found on any map.

I found myself attending a house of mourning next, a wake. The sister and father of a work friend I knew, but did not know, had passed away. Drugs had been involved in some way. Their motion-less bodies lay in open coffins. Ronald was the name of their brother, and he was a handsome, friendly young man with shoul-der-length blond hair. He was wearing a lumberjack-style jacket with red and black patches on it and a woollen lining inside. He spoke with a southern American drawl, perhaps from Texas or such, and I believe I may have once seen him in a television soap opera. I liked Ronald, but he and the deaths of his close family members no longer concerned me, as I now strongly sensed that the books I had sought throughout my entire existence were close, located in the coffin of his father, right underneath his corpse. I just had to look.

When I inevitably did check under the remains of the dead man, those forbidden literary fruits were indeed waiting for me, as if the exact intended moment of their true revealing had finally happened the way it was meant to and it was all fated to happen at this precise moment in time. I knew these books contained great unearthly power and knowledge, but I also knew how inher-ently wrong it was to read from the passages contained—I just could not help myself, however. It had become an addiction, an obsession, without me even realising it.

As I read the entirety of the dark pages in front of me, I failed to notice that everyone else in the room had disappeared com-pletely, as if they had never been there in the first place.

And so, I read and read and studied in detail the mysterious tomes that had plagued my dreams for so many years.

Eventually, I woke up.

When I awakened in my bed, I felt good, fresh even, for the first time in a long, long while, but I also had a strong feeling that some-thing important was amiss. Something had changed. Dramatically. Irreversibly.

I got out of my bed in just my boxer shorts and t-shirt and

walked outside of my front door.

There were strange, bright orange lights in the cloudless skies above as far as the eye could see. This in itself was startling, but what really shook me was the sight—or lack of, to be more precise—of what lay directly in front of me:

Belfast's Black Mountain, the main highlight of the view from my house, was no longer there. It had simply vanished, literally, like it had been swallowed up whole by the earth. Just a barren extended wasteland lay in its place. I was shaken to my very core, deeply confused, and becoming more traumatised by the second. What the fuck was going on here? Surely I was still dreaming!

But I wasn't.

Things then began to get even more unsettling. Everything around me was blurring unnaturally. Time seemed to be speeding up, then slowing down, before going faster again. Cataclysmic events were happening right around me, and I was just a mere cog in it all with no way whatsoever of controlling it.

A memory from the day before returned to me. I had watched a news report online boldly claiming that some of the world's top scientists had gotten together in secret over the last few years and after much laborious research and experimentation, were now openly claiming to have finally unlocked the complete codes of the Universe—"the DNA of the space-time continuum," as they put it—and would soon be revealing in detail exactly what they had discovered. It was going to be huge, they posed, and would change everything completely, once and for all.

What the fuck have those maniacs done? I screamed internally.

Other people soon appeared on my street in a Silverstream Parade, all just as bewildered and terrified as I.

The weather rapidly changed next: thunder, lightning, extreme hailstones one minute; dry, burning, intense heat from a bubbling, unnatural sun the next. All of space and time appeared to be folding in upon itself, as people were becoming fused with others, some even entwined with animals and inanimate objects like cars and fences.

A woman I knew from my street was approaching me, but her

features were distorting horrifically as she did—her eyes now somehow coming together and morphing into one gigantic cyclopic monstrosity right in the centre of her forehead. She grabbed onto me and screamed in desperate self-pity before falling to the ground as a six-legged dog fused with a cat stumbled past, yelping in agony, its three eyes and two mouths writhing in confused pain.

Uncontrolled madness—a screeching insanity—was everywhere around me as the extreme, opposing weather conditions continued to change on a whim and the delicate balance of the Universe became more and more broken.

I couldn't bear it any longer as my quickly weakening clasp on reality was deteriorating at an alarming rate, like trying to grasp a fistful of smoke. It soon became too much to take, and I felt myself passing out as everything faded to black.

I came to my senses lying face down on a beach of some sort. Eventually, after what seemed like an eternity—though may only have been a few seconds—I got myself together and sat up. The sky above me was a strange mix of black and a shade of purple I had never seen before. The ocean in front of me seemed to stretch on forever, but also appeared devoid of life, its waves slowly, calmly, rocking back and forth. The blood-coloured red moon in the heavens was the only source of what was a rather weak light.

I felt relaxed and at ease for some reason, despite the recent memories of what had happened. It felt like I was now in some form of Hell—or Purgatory perhaps—one made directly by the hands of the human race themselves with their overly inquisitive nature. The Christian Bible was written by men—for me there was no doubt of that, but wasn't there a verse in there somewhere that stated that too much knowledge of a certain kind was forbidden, and if discovered there would be the severest of consequences? That certainly seemed to be the case here.

As I pondered on this thought, I became aware of a commotion going on behind me. I turned to see what it was.

In the near distance, on the dusty, alien-looking dunes behind me, what resembled a giant ladybird was locked in a vicious fight to the death with another oversized insect, similar perhaps in appearance to an earwig, both creatures around the size of large horses. Their awful sounding clicking, clucking, and clashing noises while they savagely rained violent blows upon each other were truly gruesome, grotesque sights and sounds to behold. The basest of creatures, now magnified in size alongside their inhuman, cold ferociousness, were probably also completely insane, or as close to insanity as an insect can ever get.

Each too concerned with their immediate adversary, they didn't appear to notice me, and I wanted to keep it that way. I got myself together and began walking further along the beach.

I walked and walked for a very long time.

After what felt like many miles of the same empty, barren terrain ahead of me, I noticed a small, human-like figure walking towards me from far away in the darkened, bleak horizon. Maybe I had come across another survivor of the catastrophic events—like me, I thought.

As the figure came closer, I noticed it was a young boy, adorned in a black cloak and yet with no visible hair or eyebrows. He had the deepest, most mesmerizing blue eyes imaginable. He posed no apparent threat as he casually strolled right up to me and smiled in a knowing manner. I smiled back, instinctively feeling at ease in his company and asked him his name.

"I am God," the boy told me.

"Yes, I know," I replied, this realization feeling completely natural.

"This nightmare, all of this, it is all your fault. You do know this, do you not?"

"Yes, I do. And I'm sorry."

"I know you are. Please, come with me. I have something I would like you to see."

The boy took me gently by the hand and we walked together slowly through the strange sands of the beach whilst chatting like two very familiar friends that had known each other all their lives. He told me he was taking me to a place I knew very well but had never visited before. A small seaside town with a lighthouse.

As we walked hand in hand along the beach, I just knew everything was somehow going to be okay again.

LA MUERTE DE LA HUMANIDAD

This is the coastal town,
They forgot to close down.
Armageddon, come Armageddon!
Come, Armageddon! Come!
- Morrissey, "Everyday is Like Sunday"

I once heard a quote in a war film that Hell is the impossibility of reason. I disagree. For me, Hell is many things, one of them being alone and afraid somewhere alien.

I was dreaming again.

This prison filled me full of dread. I didn't even know where it was, or by extension, where *I* was. It was somewhere foreign and hot, that's all I knew. Maybe it was Hell itself.

I could almost physically feel the atmosphere, it was so tense. This was not a place of low-level, petty criminals. No, this was where the hardcore of rapists and murderers resided, and a riot was breaking out.

The four internal sides of the seemingly never-ending caged floors and cells were alive with bustling chaos. Madness was ensuing. Prisoners fought viciously with wardens and each other. Some of them were stabbing at their jailers with makeshift weapons made from toothbrushes and razor blades. I saw a prisoner slash directly across the face of an officer, crimson spurting from his gaping wound, disfigured for life if he even managed to escape this horror show with his life intact. Fierce dogs were accompanying the wardens, bloodthirsty, saliva dripping from their angry, large-toothed mouths, hungry for some human meat. A muscular, tattooed, and pony-tailed prisoner managed to break through an area of the caging surrounding the corridors and inexplicably leapt to his death, crushing onto the floor in a crunching heap of bone and flesh.

The insanity continued for what seemed like a very long time. Punchings. Kickings. Stabbings. Bitings. Heads being jumped upon. Limbs being removed. The whole place awash with blood and sinew. Debased. Humanity at its very worst. Such a violent species.

I left my cell and struggled through the sea of bodies attacking one another, eventually making it safely to the gym a few floors below. My only friend there—I think his name was Aaron—appeared and grabbed my hand, hastily demanding that I come with him as he knew where we must go to completely escape this nightmare.

We ran and made it outside to the prison yard, away from the carnage but still within the grey walls of this wretched place. What was to follow was somewhat muddled. Vague even.

A river appeared in the yard, and to reach the exit on the other side we had to cross it, like Charon himself making passage to the Ancient Greek Otherworld. Spare a coin for the ferryman, would you?

But before crossing the river, we made and ate some toast.

As we waded through the water, unusually fanged fish jumped from it and attempted to sink their sharp teeth into us. Aaron continued to hold on to my hand tightly as we struggled across, our movements tediously slow, wading heavily forward as the weird fish bit at us, breaking the flesh somewhat and causing the river below to be dyed partially red.

At last, we made it to the other side, through the exit door and into the beautiful sunshine and daylight of the outside world. We stole a bright red convertible Porsche that had belonged to one of the presumably now-butchered wardens and sped off into the countryside and freedom...

Merging seamlessly with what had gone before, I now found myself alone in a desolate wasteland.

Buildings reduced to rubble. Broken glass everywhere. Mess. Houses destroyed. The aftermath of some cataclysmic event. Society as we know it no longer existing. Ghost town. A chilling, deafening silence.

I trudged through the debris all around me. A naked child's doll stared at me from the ground with its only remaining eye, covered in dirt, its hair singed. The doll's right hand was pointing straight in front of me towards the ruined remains of what used to be family homes. I walked towards them. The sky above was on fire, all shades of dark oranges and vivid reds, combusting turbulently. The sun no longer hung in the heavens, only this terrifying, menacing, flaming, carmine skyscape. I had a knowing feeling of great trepidation deep within the very pit of my stomach. Something really bad had happened. Something irreversible. Something final.

A lone church bell sounded in the distance.

I entered the first derelict house. It was awash with dust and the remnants of what used to be a happy home—the charred remains of electrical appliances, pictures that once hung proudly on walls, a burnt-out sofa, children's toys and handheld computer games. All mod-cons now rendered completely useless and irrelevant. A group of cockroaches in the soot-filled corner scuttled over each other, making unsettling clicking noises all the while.

I entered a dining room. On what was left of a large oval dining table sat a lone bird, staring both at and through me with intentional malevolence, knowingly, its one visible large eye completely black as the darkest of dark nights. As it spread its wings magnificently, I realised it was a seagull, and a massive one at that. Its wingspan and magnitude made it appear like an epic bird of prey, or perhaps even a pterodactyl. It was sporting a black eye patch on the left side of its face, and on its beak rested an upward-pointing comedy moustache, the sort you can buy in joke shops. As it prepared to take flight, it squawked a message at me in a shrill, unearthly human tongue: "*La muerte de la humanidad!*" It then flew regally out of the glassless back window of the room and into the bleak sky above.

The ghosts then screamed out and spoke to me, relaying exactly what had happened.

The death of humanity had been a rather accelerated occurrence. No one seemed to know which country had started the war or sent the nuclear missiles in the first place; whichever madman pushed the button first was a mystery. It didn't matter in the end. When the people realised the terrible truth of what was going on, there was great screaming and weeping, a wailing and gnawing of teeth. Amid the pandemonium and confusion, doomed souls rushed to be with their loved ones, bidding hysterical farewells as the afterlife beckoned for all. Vain, futile prayers were muttered.

But maybe this is what humanity really deserved after centuries of causing untold suffering and destruction everywhere it went. A collective suicide not caused by any god or cosmic being, but at the species' very own hand. There was something ironic about it. Perhaps Aldous Huxley was right after all. Maybe this world really was another planet's hell.

Regardless, that day in the land of gods and monsters the human race went extinct, not to prideful heroics, but to a grovelling, pathetic blubbering.

This was my final dream.

THE EVIL MEN DO:
A WARNING TO THE
SELF-INDULGENT

Here comes a candle to light you to bed,
And here comes a chopper to chop off your head.
Chip chop, chip chop...
- Oranges and Lemons, traditional English nursery rhyme

What have I become, my sweetest friend?
- Nine Inch Nails, "Hurt"

There is a set of thick, majestic, jet-black curtains that hang decadently in a strange and darkened room. On these curtains appear odd, indecipherable symbols etched in a gold material. An ancient, long forgotten language? A coded form of communication by peculiar bodies of other astral plains? A forbidden tongue? No one knows. And what lies beyond the curtains? The unseen monster—pure, unadulterated evil and cruelty—and it is waiting patiently with bated breath.

This is in a world that cannot be found on any map. A place of unspeakable terror and undefined trauma. An area that exists only to torment and unleash unfounded pain in every conceivable manner. Where the demons reside.

It is only on an extremely rare occasion one can break through this dimension and escape through the barriers in between worlds and behind the edge of consciousness wherein exist other realities.

The realm, this dark place, lies within the subconscious mind of Danny Madden.

I awaken. Not from the sleep of the innocent, but that of the guilty. Six straight days and nights of nonstop drinking have left me with a devastating feeling of impending doom. I know something bad has happened, something really bad, and this situation is only going to worsen greatly. I can't quite put my finger on exactly what this bad thing is yet, due to deeply clouded, confused memory banks, as blacked out as the darkest of winter nights. I need to go for a piss so badly my groin aches, but I cannot yet muster the energy to get up and relieve myself in the toilet. Maybe I should just let loose and piss all over the bed. It wouldn't be the first time.

I look around me. I am in the small bedroom of my two-bedroom flat. Makes sense. I am naked with a dirty quilt pulled over me. The debris of the alcoholic binge fills my bedroom—empty vodka bottles, "barrack busters" of cheap white cider, empty crisp packets, dried-up spillages and cigarette burns on the long-ruined wooden floor. Ash and cigarette butts seemingly everywhere. My portable TV has taken a fall off the table and onto the floor, probably now broken. When did that happen? My phone appears to be missing, but I'm sure it will turn up somewhere. It always does. There is a neat little pool of yellow vomit in the left-hand corner of the room beside the door. Blood, too. The same blood apparently that has leaked onto my mattress. Where the fuck did that come from? There are other messes, but I'm sure you get the general picture.

I roll over in the bed and close my eyes, wishing for sleep. When you're depressed as fuck with a big spoonful of paranoia and anxiety thrown in for good measure, all you want to do is sleep for a very long time in the vain hope that when you eventually wake up, everything will be different and nice again. Like it was before, now a very long time ago indeed. I need a drink of water badly, too. My mouth and throat are dry and raw. I feel nauseous. I don't think I want to die, no, I'm too afraid to die right now, but I want God to take me away from this awful situation. It is too much to bear. I hate myself. I want to cry but cannot.

I lie like this for minutes, maybe hours, maybe even days. Every time I drink or take drugs now it takes away a little bit of my soul that can no longer be replaced.

The hangover horn is now upon me. I imagine large naked, milky white breasts bouncing over me as I am being ridden by some unknown twenty-year-old nymphomaniac blonde slut. The thought passes and soon returns to the insidious fear and my aching crotch and throat as dry as the Sahara Desert. I really need water and to relieve myself badly, but I am still too weak and scared to get up. I am existing in my own personal hell, and I am absolutely certain the Devil is waiting for me just around the corner, ready to pounce and claim his new and sweet-tasting fresh soul. A soul that was sold to him and the bottle almost twenty-five years ago. It won't be long now, I reckon.

There is no more drink left in the flat. I have a memory of desperately running out of my poison before I eventually fell into a drunken coma last night. I remember frantically phoning around all the taxi places late at night, after the off-licences and bars had closed, looking to see if any of them had any drink they could deliver—anything, really. At least one of them told me to fuck off directly, and another let me know that I was barred from their depot for life because I still owe them money for drink and for running off without paying a fare the other night. Another incident which I cannot recall.

I hate this world. Such a violent, nasty, and unforgiving place.

On this planet, there are babies born with incurable, terminal illness. Thousands of people are massacred on a whim daily for some petty squabble or another and thousands more starve to death, all while the great and the good turn a blind eye and either pretend they don't see it or try to work out an angle from which it will benefit themselves. We've all seen those ghoulish teatime adverts, after all. What sort of a loving god would allow such misery to not just exist, but to thrive? More like an impotent or non-existent deity, if you ask me. Sometimes I just wish Putin or Trump or Kimmy or whoever would push that big red button and put an end to this wretched stink once and for all. I once heard it said that we would fail to evolve as a species if we did not have our struggles, but fuck me, give me a break, please. Give us all a break, in fact. Even for the day. Just one day, that's all I ask.

I decide I will get up to relieve myself. Struggling to stand up straight, my head thumps as if there is someone banging on a Lambeg drum within. I stumble and almost fall, using the wall to steady myself. I put my hands over my face to try to bring myself around a bit. It is then when I feel the beard I now have after almost a week of not shaving. My teeth feel dirty and my breath stinks. I rustle my hair and its touch is greasy with little bits of dry skin and other detritus falling from it. I open the door and look at the landing and bathroom ahead of me. What appears to be an almost half-full plastic bottle of Frosty Jack's strong white cider is propped up against the side of the door. I don't remember noticing it before, but it may come in handy very soon.

As I walk from the bedroom to the bathroom, I notice out of the corner of my left eye something that makes me stop dead in my tracks. A wave of shock hits me first, followed by that horrible feeling of terrible realisation and memory returning. The one that reaches right into the pit of your stomach and rips out your innards. I turn and look into the open door of the main bedroom of my flat, beside the one that I just woke up in, with a terrifying glare, mouth agape whilst beginning to shake all over, immersed in a real-life horror show I have created, one that I designed mere hours earlier before ringing those taxis depots in sheer desperation for more alcohol to take away the pain—or at very least numb to it for a little while.

It is the dead body of the woman from last night.

I fall on the ground below and curl up into a little ball like I used to do as a small child. I cry loudly and punch the floor while begging God to make everything okay again, to give me a second chance, to make this horrifying event go away. I lie in this pathetic state of my own making for quite some time before calming down a little.

A thought comes. Maybe she's not really dead, but just unconscious, or even sleeping. I jump up quickly and dash into the room and shake her body, pleading with her to wake up, begging her, desperately shaking and shaking and shaking this lifeless lump of meat, but all to no avail.

She is not sleeping or in a coma. She is a corpse, as dead as the proverbial dodo. Her naked body is cold to the touch. She smells a little foul already, and there are scrapes and bruises all over her, especially on her throat and face where she is sporting two black, swollen eyes—the side effect of a freshly broken nose, reminding me of a macabre version of Robert De Niro in *Raging Bull*. I eventually realise the futility of my efforts and gently place her back on the bed and pull a quilt over her body and head. I exit the room, now practically overcome with shock and fear, and go back into the other bedroom to lie down on the bed and think, piecing together the previous night's events and what my plan of action should be next.

Her name is... was... Sharon, twenty-one years old. Or so she told me. She was a prostitute, a lady of the night I had hired for a couple of hours after getting her number from some sleazy website I had looked up on my phone. As soon as she appeared at my flat, she wouldn't shut up, bitching and whining about the state of the place and the mess I was in myself. Constantly fuckin' nagging like an old fish wife and poking fun at my appearance too, making me feel even worse about myself than I already did.

We soon had protected sex and it wasn't exactly classic stuff either. I came rather quickly, and when I did, Sharon got up and said that was it over for me and she was leaving. I said I had paid her for two hours' service, and she had to stay until those two hours were up. She told me that once you come then that's it, finished, and it was just tough shit for me. I pathetically begged her to stay, even for an hour. She was unrelenting. We argued. She lost her temper and began slapping and punching me. In turn, I went into a rage and punched her viciously around the head several times. She fell back on the bed, and I pounced on top of her body, both of us still as naked as the day we were born, and squeezed her throat extremely tightly while she kicked and flailed around in a panicked state. I kept hold of her throat in this same tightened grip until her kicking and shaking and wild movements stopped for good.

And then I let go and went to fetch myself another drink.

What am I going to do? In a lifetime of terrible things happening to me when I was drunk, this was, without a doubt, the worst of the lot. In fact, stating it is the worst of the lot is more than an understatement. I have killed someone. I am a murderer now. A killer who has cruelly robbed a young woman of her life. So what if she was a prostitute? She was still someone's daughter, a daughter whose family would soon notice her missing and come looking for her. Along with the police, eventually—no doubt about it.

I lie on my bed shaking, in some sort of heightened state of fear and shock, terrified at what I have done and what the repercussions of my vile act will be. I curse God for allowing this to happen and turning me into a lowlife alcoholic addict killer. I never wanted this sort of life! Why me? I had promise, good jobs, happy relationships, and then alcohol came along and robbed me of it all. I don't deserve this and neither did that girl Sharon. It's not fuckin' fair! I want to die along with the girl, but I'm too fuckin' cowardly to do it myself.

I'm going to have to hand myself in. There's nothing else for it. I will just be completely honest with the police and hope that the courts will have some mercy on me. I'll go to jail for a very long time, that's a certainty, but maybe, just maybe, something good will come of it one day. At least I will be sober in jail and no harm to anyone including myself. I'll do it. I'll find my phone and contact the cops. But not yet, not just yet. Before I call them, I need a drink. One final session before it is all over for me, and they take me away.

I get up and storm out onto the landing, grab the half-finished bottle of Frosty Jack's, and chug several gulps down my neck, some of it spilling down my chest. I need to put some clothes on. I go back to the small bedroom and poke through the mess until I find boxer shorts and a t-shirt. After putting them on I go to the toilet and relieve myself, which, after I am finished, along with the effects of the cider beginning to take hold, calms me somewhat. I decide to shut the door to the bedroom where Sharon's remains are and go back to the other bedroom and finish the rest of this cheap and nasty bottle of cider. What time is it anyway? It must be around midday now and I'm going to have to find some smokes around this dump too, or at least retrieve a few decent-sized butts from the ashtrays.

After about an hour, I knock back the last of the cider, and although I am feeling a lot more relaxed and clearheaded, I am going to need more drink. I have a twenty-pound note somewhere in the living room. I'll stick on a pair of jeans and trainers and once I find it, I'll head to the off-licence at the end of the street. I don't even give a fuck about my phone right now. I don't want to be in contact with anyone today anyway. When the time is right, I will find it and then phone the police and confess my heinous crime.

The short walk to the off-licence is a surreal one. I feel the passers-by are eyeing me up suspiciously, knowing full well that I have just committed some sort of unspeakable crime. It could just be my paranoia, though, and in all likelihood, they are probably only staring at me because of the disgusting physical mess I am currently in. It's such a lovely day too, lunchtime on an early Saturday afternoon (I think it's Saturday anyway). The sun is shining splendidly on this beautiful autumn day and the shoppers are making their way into town, as the crisp brown leaves litter the path ahead of me. Spring and summer are great, but surely autumn must be the most beautiful time of the year of them all. I'm going to miss enjoying little things like this when I am sent away, but it is the price I must pay for my terrible transgression.

I enter the wine lodge of sordid shame to make my filthy acquisition. The woman behind the counter, Anne, who knows me, looks me up and down and shakes her head in a combination of contempt and pity. I purchase another "barrack buster" of Frosty Jack's white piss water, a litre of cheap vodka, and a packet of cigarettes. I stare at the government health warning printed on the cigarette packet. The image vividly shows a man's open mouth with rotting yellowed and blackened teeth and huge blisters on his lips and gums. Above the picture it reads in large lettering: SMOKING CAUSES MOUTH AND THROAT CANCER. The image does not faze me in the slightest. In fact, it amuses me somewhat. I pay for my goods, exit the off-licence, and make my way back home. A funny-looking mongrel dog trots past me in the street and barks at me in a friendly manner. "Hello, dog," I reply to his silly yelps. It may be the shock of everything that has happened and most definitely related to the drink in my system, but a great calm has suddenly come over me. I am anticipating my final drink greatly before handing myself in and am now feeling almost accepting of my fate and what has gone on in my house of horrors over the past few hours.

The drink slides down like a treat. I drink the large bottle of cider first, over a few hours. I listen to music as I sit and think, looking over my life so far. A life of missed opportunities and wastage. Nothing to show for it except for lost chances, potential careers fucked up, and meaningful relationships chucked in the bin. A pointless existence, really. As a young lad I had it all in front of me, planned out. I was going to leave school at sixteen, move to the bright lights of London and become a fantasy artist. Whatever happened to that dream? It just sort of phased out over my teenage years, soon forgotten about or put down to mere childish silliness. I was pretty good at illustrating too, but I haven't done it in many years now. Maybe I'll get back into it when I am in prison.

As I polish off the last of the vaguely apple-flavoured piss water, I fetch myself a beaker for the vodka, which shall be downed straight, of course. The first beaker-full is a tough one to get down, but I'm soon getting used to it. My mind drifts to other, more off-beat notions now. I don't really feel like going to jail today after all. If only that silly accident with the girl hadn't happened. I don't deserve to go to jail. I didn't mean to kill her anyway. It was her fault for attacking me first, not to mention trying to rip me off in the first place. Like I say, an unfortunate accident. Could happen to anyone, really.

But if it really was an accident—and I believe it was—then surely I don't deserve to go to jail at all. Do I? The law will probably take a different view of events, but if I am honest and cooperative with them then hopefully, they will be sympathetic to my plight. Or maybe not.

What if I just don't tell anyone about the accident with poor Sharon and get rid of her body and any other incriminating evidence? I mean, no one has come looking for her yet. Maybe she has no one. Maybe no one will even notice her absence. It's a long shot, but it could be worth a try, for the greater good sort of thing—in that, if I make a pact with God that after today I will live a completely sober life, stick close to Him, and dedicate my life to helping others, he will protect me and keep my dark secret regarding Sharon safe from all prying eyes...

Fuck it, I'll do it!

I grab some black bin liners from the kitchen and then run to the bedroom where Sharon's corpse is and begin searching through my old stuff. I toss photographs, dusty books, and other nostalgic keepsakes out of their bags until I eventually come across the object I am looking for and the one which will aid me in my new plan—the old "Rambo" knife that John Minnis gave me back in school in second form. It seems like such a long time ago now.

I remove the quilt from Sharon's body and lift her up into my arms, feeling the coldness from her straight away and trying not to look at her messed-up dead face. The drink has given me renewed strength and determination. This will be a grisly affair, but it has to be done. If I do it quickly enough it will soon be over, and I will be able to relax at last. I carry her into the bathroom and set her naked, motionless remains into the bathtub.

Armed with the Rambo knife, which is not quite as sharp as I would like it to be, I get to work on the removal of her limbs and the bodily dismemberment ahead. I begin with the right arm. It really is tough going. The flesh itself is easy enough to get through, but the bone at the socket beside the shoulder blade is a really tough bastard and requires all my strength and endurance, leaving me lashing with sweat. It leaves not as much mess as I first expected though, which I can only presumably put down to her blood having clotted quickly after death. I do still get the odd splatter over the good white bathroom tiles, onto the floor and over myself, however.

After a final pull and tug, the arm eventually comes free from my cutting, and I fall back on the floor after it rips off in my hand. I'm out of breath due to all the hard work and decide to rest for a bit, before getting myself another beaker-full of vodka and then working on the rest. If I can remove the other arm, legs, and head, then I can place them in black bags and dump them somewhere where nobody will find them, then work on cleaning this flat from top to bottom until it is spotless and an evidence-free zone. I reckon there is no way in the world I could do this type of operation when sober, so I may as well make the most of the vodka and get it all over and done with as soon as humanly possible.

After necking the beaker of vodka, I decide to remove Sharon's head next, as I reckon the softness of the neck will be quite easy to get through with the knife. I dig deep into her throat and move the knife around before effectively sawing off her cranium. As expected, it comes off quite easily. Her decapitated head is a gruesome sight, the stuff of nightmares, so I try not to linger on it for too long and quickly put it into the black bag along with her arm.

I rest for a few seconds to catch my breath and then decide that Sharon's right leg should be next, as it is the closest to me. Then I will turn her over and remove the limbs from the other side. This is going to be a difficult one due to the obvious greater thickness of the leg bones, and despite the massive effort and strength it will take, I just have to get this morbid sideshow done and dusted sooner rather than later. So I go to work on it with haste.

As before with the arm, I saw through the flesh of the upper thigh with ease, my knife gliding through the meat. It is as anticipated when I reach the bone, however, and my endurance in sawing it off requires my greatest strength yet.

When I am about a quarter of the way through the job at hand, I suddenly feel a stiffness throughout my body, affecting, it appears, my muscles all over. I drop the knife in the bath beside the remains and fall back onto the bathroom floor in agony. My bladder and bowels give way involuntarily, leaving a degrading mess all around me on the floor. I scream in pain as my body tightens and then convulses. The convulsions become violent and go on for what appears to be a long time until they stop abruptly, and I fall back onto the messy bathroom floor once again.

As my sanity and consciousness begin to slip away, I feel an enormous bolt of guilt rushing over me. I am so, so sorry for what I have done to that poor girl. If I survive this day, I will most definitely confess all to the police when I hand myself over to them. I hate myself for what I have done. This is not me, not the real me anyway! This has been caused by the drunken waster within, the demon drink and all the hell it brings with it. Please let me make amends, dear God. Please, I beseech you—one last chance! I'll do anything to put it right. Anything at all! I'm sorry! I'm sorry! I'm sorry! I'm really, really sorry...

And then I slide out of awareness completely and everything fades to black...

I awaken with a massive jolt, leaping off my single bed like a jack-in-the-box. My white school shirt is soaking with sweat. Woah, that was fuckin' intense! I'm confused and entranced. Autumn sunlight seeps through the blinds covering my window. What time is it? I check the clock on my chest of drawers. It is situated beside a new macabre illustration I am working on. It's almost a quarter past four. Shit! I'm going to be late for my paper round.

I rush out of my room and am greeted by my mother bringing freshly ironed clothes into my sister's room.

"Why didn't you wake me?" I bark at her. "I'm going to be late gettin' down to the shop!"

"I was just coming up to wake you, son," she assures me. "When I came home from work at three you were sound asleep, completely conked out. What were you doing home from school so early anyway? Are you sick?"

"No, we got let out early for a teacher training day."

"You better not be lying to me."

"Mummy, I had this terrible nightmare that I was an old man in my forties and an alcoholic and I killed this woman. It all felt so realistic, like it was really happening."

"Ah, it was just a bad dream, son. Nothing to worry about, although maybe you shouldn't eat as much cheese as you always do!"

"It was terrifying. Really scary."

"Don't be silly. It was just a nightmare. We all have them from time to time. And you certainly don't look like you're in your forties either! For flip's sake, you haven't even turned thirteen yet!"

"What year is this, Mummy?"

"Don't be daft!"

"Please, Mummy. Just to put my mind at rest. What year is it?"

"That must have been some nightmare you had. It's 1989, of course. Now hurry up and get your papers delivered if you are going to make it to the Hallowe'en disco at the leisure centre tonight."

"Thank you!"

And with that, I grab my bright orange newspaper bag and head for the newsagent's shop, still rather dazed from that horrific dream I just had. What was that all about? It was all just so graphic and gory. Definitely a really weird one! Was it a warning or something? Who knows? One thing is for certain anyway, I know for a fact I sure won't be able to forget about that dream for a long, long time to come.

As I walk down the street to collect my *Belfast Telegraph* newspapers for the day, I remind myself that I'll have to hide that big knife John Minnis gave me at lunchtime today in a safe place where no one will ever find it.

A WOLF AT THE DOOR

New York City, October 2015

The wretched wail of the banshee is a genuinely dreadful sound and said to be the omen of great bereavement, a bringer of devilment, unholy wickedness. I believe this to be true, as, since that loathsome night of my attack, I have been regularly plagued by their death knells and awful screeches of insanity. But they never foretell my own demise, only that of the weaker of mankind.

I was just twenty-four years of age when I was assailed and left for dead, in November of 1874, while Queen Victoria was still enjoying the early years of her reign.

This is my strange story.

I: SHADOWS IN THE MOONLIGHT

November 8, 1874

It was a business trip I was on, travelling by night on an old steam train engine to the seaside port of Shannon, County Antrim, for a meeting with a particular gentleman who went by the signature of Mr. R. Townsley. As an up-and-coming lawyer for Dobson & Son legal firm, the nature of our enterprise concerned a divorce request by a brother of Mr. Townsley, who was trapped in a loveless marriage, and according to his elder sibling, did not seem to have much of an interest in the female form. Back in those more conservative days, divorce, and most certainly homosexuality, were frowned upon, with the latter still illegal according to the laws of the land.

We had arranged to rendezvous at seven p.m. at a local restaurant going by the exotic name of Xanadu. The finer details had been ironed out in telegram communications. Alas, I never made it to the eatery. Following a hard day of sorting out tedious paperwork and administrative duties at work and a sleepless night prior, I dozed on the train and missed my stop. This was an unforgettable act of fate that would change my life prodigiously for the coming decades.

It was the driver who awakened me at the end of the line. I woke with a startled jump from my dreams—colourful visions of an apocalyptic nature: fire, brimstone, and frogs raining from the heavens, along with rivers and oceans saturated with the blood of many, including my wife and newborn daughter.

The elderly operator whose breath reeked of whiskey informed me that this was the end of the line and if I wanted to reach Shannon I would have to do so on foot, as he and his steam convoy were knocking off for the night. He advised me to head to the nearby beach, turn right and keep walking for about three miles in the direction of the Shannon lighthouse until I finally reached the town of my destination. Being already late for my conference with Mr. Townsley, I decided I would check into a local bed and breakfast for the night and catch up with him in the morning, hoping he would not be too upset with my missing our appointment.

It was a bitterly cold late autumn night, and the lack of clear visibility made things quite treacherous, although the full moon in the celestial sphere above did help a little, casting misshapen, odd shadows along the way. I could hear, though barely see, what was apparently the enormous waves of the Atlantic Ocean crashing and walloping against each other. A thick mist soon settled on the beach, making it near impossible to view far in front of me. I believe it was at this point I heard for the first time the abominable screams of what I now know to be the calling of the most gruesomely wretched of creatures, the bringers of darkness and annihilation—the banshees.

I would continue to hear their nightmarish whine many, many times over the years which were to follow.

Now slightly perturbed and fearful of these unfamiliar cries of the damned, I broke into a slight run, desperate to make it to Shannon in one piece as soon as humanly possible. But my anxious galloping flight and lack of proper visibility due to the horrendous weather conditions caused me to trip on an unseen and rather large rock on the sand.

As I lay pathetically on the seaside shore, covered in muddied sand and seaweed, I noticed that not only could I hear the awful yelps of the banshees, but there was now what appeared to be some sort of massive animal—a giant, considerable dog, I reckoned at the time—in the close vicinity. I could hear it grunting, snarling, and spitting, seemingly at close quarters to me and gaining ground. Almost in sync with the banshees, it howled its terrible howl at the moon in the starlit heavens of the dark sky overhead.

After awkwardly stumbling onto my feet again and spitting out salt-flavoured mud and sand laced with stinking weeds, I made into another sprint, this time even more out of breath and desperate, now in real fear for my life, soon giving way to an adrenaline rush of sheer panic. But the foul, savage, four-legged beast was much faster than I could ever be, and it soon caught up with me. It lunged in my direction, huge claws and sharp, elongated razor-like teeth shining brightly in the moonlight, dragged me onto the ground below, and began ripping into and mauling my pink, tender flesh, leaving me for a corpse and a proper bloodied mess.

The last thing I remembered before passing out and waking up in the hospital four months later was the monstrosity biting into my stomach and dining on some of my innards, while the devilish banshees shrieking in the background, in apparent delighted glee.

II: OF ALL THE AWFUL CREATURES

When I eventually awoke from my coma, the doctors in Belfast reported that my survival and unusually speedy recovery was nothing short of a proper miracle. They dutifully relayed to me that I had been found the following morning by an elderly female, out for a morning stroll. I was unidentifiable as a human being, looking like what merely appeared to be a massive lump of thick, dried blood and flesh, with some ripped and strewn clothing thrown in for good measure. My left arm had been hanging on by a literal thread with the rest of me—my face, torso, and legs—mutilated in what appeared to be a beyond-repair situation.

Astonishingly, however, a faint heartbeat was felt, and I was quickly rushed to the nearby hospital in Coleraine, then later on to a more sizeable one in Belfast, where they sewed me back up again, including my heavily shredded arm, in the best way possible.

Believing that I would be horrifically scarred and traumatized for life, the medics were in awed shock at the rate of my recuperation and healing, the scars soon disappearing over a very short period and my internal organs back to almost full capacity and working order. I was becoming quite the medical marvel and wonder to all, with medical experts from all over Ireland and the British Empire coming to visit to see with their own two eyes the amazing healing man that I now was.

A policeman came to visit me once, advising that my assault had more than likely been carried out by some sort of escaped big cat—a panther or cheetah perhaps—illegally acquired somewhere in deepest darkest Africa or Asia and smuggled home by boat. I wasn't so sure though, and after another fortnight or so of their tiresome, laborious prodding and examining, I decided to discharge myself from the hospital, much to the discontent of the so-called experts around me. My loving wife and baby girl had frequently visited me during my prolonged stay at the infirmary, but it was time to head for home and attempt to put this ghastly incident behind me, once and for all.

It was April of 1875 when I returned home to my humble terraced abode on Belfast's Shankill Road. My better half, Evelyn, and baby daughter, Liza, seemed delighted to have me returned to where I belonged and made a right fuss over me. In just a few days' time, with my wounds still healing at a tremendous and inexplicable pace, I planned to return to work, having made the proper arrangements with Mr. Dobson, who reassured me that he was very excited to have his highly competent deputy back in the line of duty. The only slight aftereffect of my vicious encounter that evening by beast unknown was being regularly returned to the scene of the crime in dreams and night terrors. They would soon cease entirely according to my local general practitioner who, as flabbergasted as he was at my remarkable speed of rehabilitation, expected me to make a full and proper recovery, just as the doctors at the hospital had advised him.

All things considered, everything at the time seemed a little bit too good to be true. This was not to last, however, and on the eve of my return to the workplace, my case took a wholly unexpected turn.

On the clear spring night of my metamorphosing for the first time, I had gone to bed early, in anticipation of an early rise in the morn. Sleep eluded me nonetheless, and I tossed and turned for a couple of hours before darkness, as the new full moon enveloped all around this part of the planet.

It began with a temperature and extreme pain in the forehead and my knocking back several glasses of water in a vain attempt to dispel the throbbing agony. I vomited violently next, and flu-like symptoms appeared to invade my body. The physical change began soon after, and everything that followed was an abhorrent dreamlike vision, to be forever etched in my memory banks.

Dark, thick, long hair sprouted all over my skin, the main trunk of my body expanding alongside burly, husky muscles now quickly developing on my arms, legs, and chest. My bedtime attire could not deal with the pressure, and my pyjamas soon ripped under the strain. The sheer discomforting irritation from all this change and movement was excruciatingly torturous.

Deeply panicked, I darted to the mirror on the bedside cabinet, clambering and aching everywhere all the way. A never-to-be-forgotten, starkly chilling image stared back at me from the other side of the looking glass: the face of a wolf, with dark yellow-green eyes, hair and apparent whiskers everywhere, and a set of enormous piercing fangs sprouting from my mouth cavity.

Intense cravings and a psychological obsession with raw meat overcame me. I was no longer myself and desperately longed for the basic, uncooked flesh of mammals—and human brawn would do just fine. Before departing the bedroom to consume my midnight supper, an unsettlingly familiar noise shrilled from the entry outside the window. The banshees had returned, and the awful yell and hoot of their precursor to eternal rest were deafening to me, although they had not roused my dearly beloved Evelyn, who was sound asleep in the front bedroom with my little angel. My animal instincts overpowered me, and I exited the room to go feast on the fat of my family.

Evelyn was dead before she could realize in full the sheer insanity of what was going on around her—the cutting of her throat with my vast, newly sprouted claws had seen to that.

The child was now awake and watched helplessly from her cot, clutching tightly to her beloved teddy bear, sobbing, unnerved, but not quite understanding what this thing was in front of her, chewing and consuming her mama's brains and head, with blood and little pieces of skull splashing everywhere. I continued to down what was left of my former wife's remains, munching and chomping on sinew and tendons, and even the odd bone.

After devouring everything I could of my spouse, I turned my attention and bloodlust to the infant. I was more animal than man now, but something from deep inside of me—buried underneath the dark recesses of my wolf-man hybrid psyche—would not let me harm my little princess in any way. Part of me, the part that was a monster, wanted to bite into this potential snack in front of my eyes, but the other part, perhaps the last remnants of my humanity, still loved her endlessly and could not—*would* not—harm a single hair on her brow. So, I turned on my brutish heels and departed my home for the very last time by the back door.

In the entry, I was greeted by the hysterical celebrations of those ugly, green, deformed banshees. I replied in the only way that came naturally to me. I howled ferociously at the moon in the black curtain above, the blood dripping from my claws appeared quite dark in the moonlight.

That night I killed five other innocent souls as I fled for the relative sanctuary of the nearby hills of the Glencairn part of town, including a couple of neighbours who had foolishly come outdoors to investigate the commotion at my homestead.

I roamed those hills for most of the night until I gradually became tired, falling unconscious, and waking up later the next morning naked, cold, and full of overwhelming guilt and shame.

I believed there would be a great manhunt by the police and locals for me, hellbent on vengeance, eventually making their capture and setting a date for me with the noose for the murder and cannibalizing of six undeserving victims. It was not to be, though.

Due to my absence from the crime scene at my house on the Shankill Road, I was presumed dead, eaten by the wild, rabid dog or wolf that was responsible for the appallingly frenzied slaughter. No one was looking for me. I did not know this until much later, but in my confusion, dismay, and fear, I managed to steal some clothes and made it to Belfast Harbour. I eventually stowed away on a vessel headed for Liverpool, then trekked on foot all the way down through England to the port of Dover, departing on a ship bound for mainland Europe and apparent safety.

III: THE LURKER IN YOUR MIDST

New York City, October 2015

At one hundred and sixty-five years old, I am very possibly the oldest living human being in current existence and still look as young as I did on that mid-nineteenth century day when my affliction first manifested itself, if not younger.

Over the decades, I have travelled the entirety of most of the modern world at least three times over, Western Europe and North America being my favourite stops. I am always on the move and never stay in one place for more than a month. Contrary to popular belief, a legitimate, one hundred percent full moon only occurs for a brief instant each month, but it is enough to transform me into my alter ego, the homicidal man-wolf crazed by blood and flesh.

Throughout the ages, I have sliced up and devoured—often still alive—countless unsuspecting people, well into the hundreds, although I cannot be certain and have probably lost count. I am unable to stop but have learned to live with my curse and deal with my unholy needs, still manically howling and barking at the lunar body at times, even when fully human.

I never did find out what became of my only surviving offspring, my lovely, adorable daughter, Liza. More than likely, she was adopted and had a change of name, never remembering what really happened to her biological parents on that tragic night of woeful horror. Whatever way she turned out, I hope she led a full and happy life. I might even have some great-grandchildren out there somewhere, scattered across the world.

I live quite the extravagant, multicultural lifestyle now too, and to fund it, I have become rather adept at con-artistry and swindling, having never once been brought to book for my countless wrongdoings, either as man or monstrosity. The inhuman-type behaviour of my sort is very hard to prove. My DNA and genetic makeup appear to be very rare indeed, probably completely unique. This is due to the fact that, after I was first set upon by the original wolf-creature on the Shannon beach in 1874, I am the only one I know of, after painstaking research, to become just like my antagonist instead of dying a wretched, harrowing death, like all of my own victims have.

Indeed, suffice it to say, I am a lurker in your midst, a werewolf with a curious relationship to the moon, followed and worshipped at night by an insane cult of hideous banshees—still very much at large, and with no intention of ceasing my carnal pleasures just yet.

PITCH & TOSS

If you can bear to hear the truth you've spoken
Twisted by knaves to make a trap for fools,
Or watch the things you gave your life to, broken,
And stoop and build 'em up with worn-out tools...
- Rudyard Kipling, "If"

January 1976

It was a typically gloomy, depressing winter afternoon in Belfast. The mischievous gods in the heavens above were having a laugh at the expense of the wretched humans below again, pissing down relentlessly on them from a great height, as the winds howled dementedly like a pack of wolves in distress and the cold chill air bit viciously like a piranha. Not exactly ideal weather for a game of soccer, especially one on such a waterlogged, overgrown, and poorly kept pitch as this one was.

The soggy, though admittedly welcome and refreshing, half-time oranges were passed around by the boys of Edwin Manor High School under-twelves football team, juice dripped down their red and black jerseys just as Mr. Harding was giving the lads a right bollocking. Spittle hurtled from under his impressive, though somewhat unnecessary, handlebar moustache, giving his countenance the appearance of an angry cowboy, albeit a rather camp one, minus the Stetson, and adorned in a dark green track-suit top and inappropriately revealing, tight blue shorts. His muscled, hairy, ex-athlete's legs were not unlike those of a gorilla found in the wild. His curly head of locks could also have done with a good trim.

Harding was unhappy with the boys for dropping their single-goal lead in this vital cup match against cross-community rivals St. Malachy's, now 2-1 down to the team in white, with a player from each side being sent off. Bad-tempered striker Geordie Brown had intentionally kicked an opposition player in the privates when going for the ball, adding the not-so-eloquent quip of "Fenian bastard" as the boy fell. When the lad, named Padraig, dropped, he quickly leapt to his feet again, in an act of bravado to save face, and punched Geordie square in the jaw, accompanying it with his own insult of "dirty orange fucker." The rest of the players from both sides then got involved in a scuffle that was eventually broken up by Mr. Harding and the teacher from St. Malachy's, who was refereeing. Pupils from each school spectating were reveling in the drama.

The second half soon got underway, the Edwin Manor lads briefed in no uncertain terms about what was expected of them by their football coach and P.E. teacher.

Harding's harsh words seemed to work, however, as centre-half John Gamble quickly pulled a goal back for Edwin Manor with a penalty after winger Mark Whitten was brutally fouled in the St. Malachy's box, their player receiving a yellow card for his efforts. Gamble slotted the penalty away tidily in the bottom left-hand corner after sending the goalkeeper the wrong way.

The rest of the second half was a hard-fought contest, the rough tackles flying in from both sides, young tempers often fraying. With just a few minutes remaining, St. Malachy's conceded a corner kick and Jonny Henry headed the winner for Edwin Manor with aplomb, resulting in great jubilation from his teammates and, of course, Mr. Harding. Edwin Manor was into the next round of the Schools' Cup.

The celebrations continued after the final whistle was blown and the victorious boys headed back to the pavilion changing rooms to get cleaned up before the walk home, which usually involved a sly cigarette or two in the abandoned mill for some of them.

The changing rooms weren't exactly the cleanest in the world either, mould and other general dirt a seemingly permanent fixture on the walls, ceiling, and floor, made even worse as the boys entered with their muddied, wet football boots, resulting in an ever-increasing sea of light-brown-coloured water swimming around them. Regardless, the enthusiastic lads soon removed their boots and kits and entered the communal showers to scrub off the muck and grass from the game.

As he sometimes did on occasions like this, Mr. Harding also removed his clothes and joined the boys in the showers.

Because Pete Harding quite enjoyed the company of young boys of a certain age.

His excuse, as always, was that he needed to freshen up anyway before dinner later with his wife and teenage daughters and that he wanted to keep his Ford Cortina clean on the way home too, of course.

Unlike his mind.

As the budding young footballers gradually made their way out of the pavilion, laughing and joking about their plans for the evening, their teacher was soon left alone in the changing rooms, shaving his stubble in the misty mirror above one of the long benches beside where the lads had just occupied, topless, with a maroon towel covering his lower regions. He was looking forward to his sausages and mash this evening, followed by a few beers and a bit of telly. He hoped his wife wouldn't be looking for any sex later on.

After administering some cheap aftershave to his freshly shaved face, he began dressing again, but as he was seated on the bench pulling on his socks, he was interrupted by the sound of the main door of the pavilion opening again. One of the lads must have forgotten something, he reckoned, but after a quick look around the changing room he didn't notice anything any of them might have left behind.

Determined footsteps next, moving with haste in his direction.

A slim figure opened the door of the changing room and entered. It was a youngish man, early twenties possibly, dressed in jeans and a white t-shirt. He seemed upset, angry even, and had something hidden behind his back. He seemed familiar to Harding, though. Yes, he definitely recognised that handsome face with its dark features, but it had matured slightly now, grown up. His name was Jim, possibly. Or maybe Philip. He was a former pupil at the school, for sure. One that Harding had gotten to know quite well during his earlier days at Edwin Manor, just like all the others.

The young man seemed to be staring at Harding with a profound rage and was shaking at the same time. The teacher stared back, knowing full well what was up. He knew this day was going to arrive at some point but had never really prepared for it. Eventually, the visitor spoke up.

"I've been watching you for a very long time now."

"Do I know you? Have we met before?" replied Harding.

"Oh, you fuckin' know me, you dirty fucking nonce. You ruined my life, you sick fucker."

"I think you've got me mixed up with someone else, son. And who the hell do you think you are storming in here like this? This is a school, private property. Get the fuck out of here now, you insolent little bastard, before I either call the police or kick the shit out of you myself right here and now!"

Harding stood up aggressively, thrust out his chest, and clenched his fists. The young man just smiled with a knowing intent.

A now nervous and visibly upset Harding continued. "What's your name, son? What's this all about anyway? Is it about money? Are you looking to rob me? Is this an attempt at blackmail or something?"

"Oh, you know my name all right. Jim Reilly. Remember?"

"No, I don't know you at all, son. Get the fuck out of here before I have to teach you a lesson you won't forget."

"You don't remember me? How about I jog your memory then? Like those times you used to make me wait behind after detention? Or how about when you used to give me a lift home after games every Wednesday? Those detours you used to make? Those awful things you used to pay me to do for you in that horrible car of yours? Do you remember those? *Do ya*, ya dirty fuckin' bastard?"

"You're out of your mind. You'll never be able to prove any of that to anyone. Take yourself off right now and we'll forget this little incident even happened today."

Harding watched as Jim Reilly removed from behind his back what he had been hiding. It was a football sock, stretched downwards due to the heavy objects contained inside of it. The three snooker balls within clinked as they made contact with each other.

Realising what was about to happen, Harding took a lunge at his former pupil, but Jim easily dodged out of the way of the teacher's punch. He took a further step back and then swung the snooker balls in the sock above his head with great velocity before crashing them violently against the side of Harding's head, which caved in immediately, the old schoolmaster's shocked and trembling body dropping to the tiles of the changing room floor below with a dense thud. Deep red gushed from the injury as the man's body convulsed while Jim calmly—driven by a sheer, focused, seething wrath—finished off the job, raining blow after blow on top of the head of his abuser with the snooker balls in the sock until all that remained of it was little bits of pulped sinew and brains.

Harding's blood coalesced on the tiled floor with the muddied water from earlier, forming a new shade of red-brown, before flowing across the tiles and down the drain.

June 1978

Both in their early twenties and both fuelled by a rather substantial amount of alcohol, Sandra and Davy had just met in The

Crescent nightclub, a dark, dingy place that specialised in Goth music and cheap liquor. Davy had been instantly attracted to Sandra's long dark hair and voluptuous body, although he wouldn't have put it in quite the same terms. He'd asked her if she wanted to accompany him on a late-night drive in his car, which was parked just outside the disco. He told her he knew of a nice quiet spot at the back of his local park where they could be alone and chat. After a bit of mild hesitation, Sandra relented and the two of them stumbled outside arm in arm to Davy's souped-up light blue Capri.

The potential lovebirds parked in a remote spot just behind the park bandstand, the summer sun setting in the luminous, multicoloured sky above. The weather was hot and sticky, and so was Davy. They lit up a cigarette in unison, both drawing on it heavily, and blew the smoke out of each of the opposing rolled-down windows where they were seated. They chatted for a brief while about their lives and jobs, both bored with where they were headed in life and looking for some fresh, new, and exciting adventures to embark upon. There was chemistry. It felt good and right.

Davy was about to make his move when...

A low-sounding noise, a muffled wail perhaps. Was that crying? Yes, definitely the sound of what seemed to be a man weeping. Then screaming. Louder and louder.

Sandra and Davy pulled away from each other with a look of surprise and apprehension etched upon their faces. They stared out of the front window of the car in an attempt to see where the sounds were coming from, but to no avail.

More wailing and distorted words. Almost certainly a male voice.

Without saying a word, Davy opened the door and carefully stepped out of the car to investigate, Sandra following him shortly afterwards as the cries and rambling sounds got closer and closer.

They soon found the source of all the commotion at the back of the bandstand. The man was a wreck, completely dishevelled, rolling around the ground screaming and in floods of tears, a raving thing, babbling incoherently about ghosts and debts being paid in full.

The couple helped the deeply distressed, shabbily dressed man to his feet and after some discussion decided they would take him to the nearest hospital for help.

As they threw the man's arms over their shoulders and attempted to drag him back to the car, Sandra noticed a slight movement in the corner of her eye within the trees, just to the side of the bandstand. It was a dark figure, a shade, seemingly watching what they were doing intensely. The figure had a handlebar moustache and was dressed in a green tracksuit top and blue shorts. She found it odd and more than a little unnerving, but once she had turned around fully to face the figure it was gone just as quickly as it had appeared.

Davy and Sandra drove the man, who was clearly suffering from some sort of mental breakdown, to the hospital which quickly admitted him, the staff there soon sending the couple on their way. It was only on a later date that they learned of his name: James Andrew Reilly. They also discovered that the hospital had sectioned him to a psychiatric facility on the outskirts of Belfast.

October 2020

Jim Reilly remained in a secure psychiatric unit until his passing at the age of sixty-five from a viral infection in the early weeks of autumn 2020. He had spent the majority of his adult years institutionalised. Shortly after his original admission to hospital in 1978, he confessed to, and was charged with, the murder of schoolteacher Peter Harding, who himself was revealed to be a notorious serial paedophile and abuser of young boys under his guard at Edwin Manor High School.

Jim Reilly was declared unfit for trial, however, due to his severe mental deterioration. Constantly, until his death, he claimed that he was tormented by the ghost of the man he had killed, a vengeful spirit whom, he was adamant, would never allow him to rest until his own passing. He had been tortured all his life by Harding, while the abuser was both alive and dead.

But there had always been one glimmer of hope for Jim Reilly. Despite the living hell he went through at the hospital for over forty years, there was always that one thought that got him through even the darkest of days.

Because of his violent actions on that fateful day in January 1976, he had ended the reign of terror Pete Harding had inflicted on many innocent children over several decades, dating back to the 1940s. Jim had stopped him dead in his tracks—literally. Because of Jim, countless children had undoubtedly been saved from a cycle of horrific abuse at the P.E. teacher's hands. Yes, he had paid a very heavy price for his own crime, but, for him, it was a price worth paying.

He had destroyed a monster.

Jim Reilly was finally at peace.

THE DEVIL CAME AND TOOK ME

Hey diddle diddle,
The cat and the fiddle,
The cow jumped over the moon.
The little dog laughed,
To see such fun,
And the dish ran away with the spoon.
- Traditional nursery rhyme

Late January 2008

*B*eing sober is being forced to conform to society's imposed norms. One becomes enslaved to an unemotional and unattractive machine, mere cogs in a system of creative and intellectual oppression that does not love us back. This is of particular relevance to the working classes. The only real releases from this waking nightmare are to get regularly, intentionally out of one's proverbial tree on mood-altering substances and, of course, death itself, but as Irvine Welsh once so sagely stated, death will probably be shite, too. Going on a massive fuck off hedonistic bender for a few days and nights, involving alcohol and illegal drugs, is a massive two-fingered salute to this selfish integral organisation of orderliness—and it feels pretty damn good, in several ways. In short, fuck the system.

These were just some of the racing thoughts slipping through Stevie Brown's mind that day as he left his place of employment on a half-day pass.

Stevie hated his job at the call centre. He particularly detested those stupid, ignorant, whiny, rude, dumb-fuck members of the public who called in to him every day, with their incessant idiotic questions and complaints of a highly tedious and easily-resolved nature. The general public were major league assholes; in fact, he pretty much loathed the vast majority of the human race, save for one or two rare exceptions. As Stevie headed to the nearest bar he could find, more thoughts filled his head.

Life is not a film, nor a book of fiction. It is very real and any bad decisions you make will have serious repercussions which can sometimes take many years to become realised. You reap what you sow. A happy ending is never guaranteed. In fact, when you really think about it, since all our lives will end in death and whatever idea of Heaven or Hell each individual has in their mind is definitely not a certainty, then technically every life has an unhappy ending. That said, there can be good, even great, times in between, but you really are the author of your own destiny, so try your very hardest not to fuck it up, despite what fate has bestowed upon you. Being an alcoholic and/or addict is far from a glamorous existence, despite what many idiotic wankers will have you believe. Addiction to mood-altering substances, whatever your drug of choice may be, will degrade you in the extreme—you will do things that in sobriety would both shock and disgust you. But this not being enough, you will continually return to the scene of the crime for more of the same in a seemingly continuous, never-ending loop until there is a break in the cycle, through either an epiphany of clarity or the aforementioned death. Now, that is insanity, or at the very least some form of personality disorder.

There is, of course, always a choice every time the addict/alcoholic is faced with this dilemma in the form of cravings or otherwise, despite how greyed and muddied the waters can very often appear. Two-year-old children diagnosed with leukemia or born with HIV don't have a choice, but the addict will often happily ignore the fact that he has a choice and continue to wallow in his selfish desires and self-pity. His or her self-destructive nature is something of a pleasure to behold to them, however, in that whatever madness and pain lies in front of them is well deserving in their minds. And the temporary numbing of their pain is well worth it for a short period of euphoria. One thing they are promised, however, is many future years—if they survive long enough, that is—filled with un-happiness, depression, and regret, looking back over a life of "what could have beens." Every single choice we make in this life will therefore define the quality—or lack thereof—of our remaining time on this dying planet, climaxing with that previously referenced unhappy ending. So choose wisely.

Despite knowing much better than what most others in his shoes do, Stevie entered the first bar he got to anyway. He'd also decided somewhere along the line that he had just quit his job for good this time.

Hunter's bar on the Lisburn Road area of South Belfast was the nearest to the call centre and it would do just rightly. It wasn't a bad joint really. Just like the area where it was based, it could probably be best described as working class trying to be middle class. Quite the multi-cultural area of the city too, it is also home to a large student populace, many of them being educated at the close by Queen's University. It's a pretty nice area actually and the perfect place for an alcoholic to frequent for a nice quiet pint or twenty, away from the hustle and bustle of the main city centre and certain "local" bars on all sides of the political persuasion, full to the brim with paramilitaries and wankers. Stevie even had his own name for the district—"Studentville"—and he certainly didn't have a problem drinking anywhere that sold his particular brand of poison. Over the years, he'd drank in almost every part of the town (a spot of cross-community partying never bothered him at all!) and further afield. But these days, when he did decide to go on a bender, he just wanted somewhere quiet with a jukebox where nobody knew him. The fact that his workplace was located in such an area was even more convenient, for good and bad.

The first couple of pints were bliss and were downed rather quickly indeed (as per usual). Stevie could relax properly now, his mind becoming more at ease, enjoying himself more as his inhibitions slowly but surely slithered away. Until the inevitable nightmare gradually began, of course, one that is always in the post the moment the first drink is taken.

As the youngish man (Stevie was now in his early thirties) got up to put on a few tunes on the jukebox he noticed a handsome man with dark hair, eyes, and features—on first appearance in his early fifties—watching him select his songs from the machine with flashing lights. Stevie didn't really pay much attention to him, though. He was more concerned about his musical choices. He was in the mood for a bit of Oasis, to remind him of his relatively youthful days back in the 1990s.

As Noel Gallagher was crooning about making Sally wait and not looking back in anger, Stevie's mind relaxed even more, the chemicals from the alcohol already in his system helping him on his voyage through the temporarily extremely contented stage of the binge, now at true peace with the universe, everything at last making sense—worries, trials and tribulations now long gone. The key word here being temporary, the heightened state of nirvana never lasting.

Another couple of pints of Harp lager later, Stevie decided it was almost time to go on the cider. To him, there was nothing quite like a delicious glass of fermented apples with ice. An acquired taste, yes, but for the cider connoisseur like him these moments were to be cherished.

Jarvis Cocker was now emanating from the music system, performing Pulp's "Razzmatazz," as Stevie sat down with his sweet-tasting glass of apple-based beverage. He thought to himself how underrated a band Pulp was back in the mid-'90s. His tipsy notions then reverted to his childhood days of stage magic.

As a pre-teen he was a keen amateur magician, learning the

tricks of the trade through books and magic sets, often given to him as Christmas or birthday presents. He was a regular customer of the local town centre joke shops, too. When he and his family used to holiday at his uncle's caravan in County Down, Stevie would perform magic shows for them at night, dazzling all and sundry with his mysterious, inexplicable card tricks and sleight of hand. He now regretted not continuing with this hobby into adulthood. Who knows where it may have taken him? Perhaps performing shows all over the world, like David Blaine or Paul Daniels, the latter of whom he used to watch as a kid. He would probably now even have become an esteemed member of the illustrious "Magic Circle." But when those awkward teenage years came, his love of the shocking and entertaining of audiences soon faded. There was also that little incident in the Isle of Man when he was thirteen and away on his holidays once more with his family.

At the time he considered himself too old to be doing things with his mum, dad, and two younger sisters, so he wandered around Douglas on his own for a lot of the holiday and one night wound up at a hypnotist's show in some old Victorian theatre building. When the hypnotist was looking for volunteers from the audience to be brought on stage and put in a trance, Stevie excitedly put up his hand and was selected alongside a few other willing punters game for a laugh.

Alas, it was soon to be discovered first hand by the young lad that the hypnotist was indeed a fraud, and this disappointment had a profound effect on him, in part fuelling his deep cynicism with the world in his adult years. Expecting to be properly put into a trance and mentally controlled by the showman, Stevie was never really hypnotised at all by the man and simply played along with his commands for two reasons—to placate the intimidating hypnotist and also because he was on stage in front of a considerable audience so felt the necessity to perform, in this particular case pretending he could see a monkey chasing him around the stage. Monkey business indeed. The next day, when he bumped into a bunch of older guys in their twenties from Dublin who recognised him from his stage antics and whose friend was also one of the audience members brought to the stage, they relayed to him that their friend also wasn't really hypnotised either, confirming Stevie's suspicions that the hypnotist was indeed one big fat liar and fake.

Stevie went outside in the cold winter afternoon for a smoke, the new ban on smoking in public places now well in place. It was just beginning to snow as some Goth youths passed him at the front of the bar and after some conversing amongst each other, they finally decided to go into Hunter's for a drink also. Stevie reckoned if he ever did get back into stage magic, he would hire a Goth girl as his glamorous assistant. Goth girls were so fucking sexy to him, with their colourful hairstyles, extreme piercings, strange tattoos, and slutty, revealing outfits. Once he finished his cigarette he tossed it onto the pavement, stood on it, and went back inside to go for a piss before returning to his drink.

As he stood at the urinal relieving himself, Stevie couldn't help but feel he was being watched by a man who had followed him into the toilet and was now standing beside the sink. It was the darkly featured chap whom he had noticed earlier sitting on the other side of the bar, drinking presumably whiskey or some sort of other spirit in a small glass. After finishing his piss and buttoning up his jeans, Stevie turned around to find that this weird man was indeed staring at him intently, watching his every move. Stevie decided upon an attempt at breaking the awkwardness.

"Hello there. How's it going?"

No reply. Just more intense staring.

"Are you okay, mate? What's the deal here? Have you got some sort of problem or what?"

The man eventually spoke in an odd, dreary tone.

"Sorry. My apologies. I've just been watching you for a bit, that's all. No harm intended. You caught my attention when you first came into the bar, and I've been watching you ever since. Sorry, where are my manners? Pleased to meet you. My name is Augustus."

Augustus held out his hand for Stevie to shake. Stevie nervously, gently shook it back.

"Good to meet you too, Augustus, but what were you staring at me for? What's that all about then? Look, if this is what I think it is, then I have to say I'm flattered but I'm just not that way inclined. Anyway, look after yourself. I'm away for another liquor here."

As Stevie exited the small, confined toilet with his back to Augustus, the man chased after him, halting him by placing his hand tightly on his right shoulder, forcing Stevie to spin around.

"Look, look, let me buy you a drink. I promise you it's not what you think, not at all. I think I might know you from somewhere, that's all. That's why I was staring at you. Sorry if I freaked you out a bit. I mean you no harm. Please, let me buy you a drink to apologise."

"Listen, mate. Don't worry about it, honestly. No biggie, no harm done. Don't worry about the drink either."

Stevie actually wanted to accept the offer of the drink, as he didn't have that much money on him, and for his binge to continue as he planned, he was going to have to phone someone to borrow some cash pretty soon. He was simply faking politeness until the guy inevitably asked him again.

"Look, I don't mind, I really don't. And I honestly think I do know you from somewhere. Look, I'm having a Jack Daniels on the rocks. Do you want one too?"

"Okay then, you've twisted my arm. Make mine a Jack and white lemonade though. I'll be sitting over in the corner there."

"Coming right up. Oh, by the way, what's your name?"

"Stevie."

"Good to meet you, Stevie. I'll be two shakes of a lamb's tail."

As Augustus went to the bar to order the drinks, Stevie went back to his seat wondering if this was such a good idea after all. Maybe he should just have the one drink with the man and then split. He just wanted to be alone and get out of his tree anyway. Perhaps he should head for home, get a lend of more money from someone and purchase a massive carry-out, which would do him well into tomorrow.

Augustus soon returned with the drinks, and they got chatting again.

The two men talked for more than an hour over a few rounds of drinks, tedious small talk at first, followed eventually by a conversation of more substance. They both spoke of their shared hatred of their jobs. Augustus explained that he was an English professor at Queen's University and how the job was beginning to drain him, physically and mentally. He had nothing but contempt for his bureaucratic superiors (only interested in statistics and money) and the current batch of students studying at the well-respected place of learning. Stevie spoke to the strange Augustus about how he had just walked out of his job at the call centre, having simply had enough of stupid fuckers hurling abuse at him over the phone line and his whiny little manager, Scott Large.

"I don't blame you, Stevie. I couldn't stick it in one of those places either. All that abuse and nonsense you have to put up with. No way."

"Yea, and for really shitty pay too."

"Minimum wage?"

"Not a kick in the arse off it."

"No, it wouldn't be my scene. At least you don't have to put up with a bunch of spoilt millennials with a self-entitlement complex. So, what are you going to do with yourself now?"

"What's a millennial when it's at home?"

"The youth of today. Kids born after 1985 or the like. 'Generation Y.' I believe it has something to do with a bunch of murders that happened to some kids in America back then. Ever since that event, children in general there were mollycoddled and overprotected much, much more. They were told that whenever they grew up, they could be literally whatever they wanted and go into any field of work they wished, which, as you know, is nonsense. They were only told positive stuff about themselves, the 'everyone gets a medal' sort of attitude, where they were never properly shown how to deal with failure in life in their formative years, resulting in a new generation of adults who genuinely believe they are entitled to everything they want. Without the laborious hard work, time, and effort, of course. As per usual, these attitudes transferred across the Atlantic. It's not actually the fault of the kids that they are such self-obsessed brats. The problem lies with their parents and society as a whole. The emergence of the Internet, instant messaging, and so on has made things even worse, as they now not only demand everything they want, but they demand it all straight away. So anyway, enough of my incessant ramblings; what are your plans now that you have quit your job?"

"Ah, I get you now. Thank fuck I grew up as a member of 'Generation X' then. I dunno. I'll be on the piss for a few days now, borrowing and begging, no doubt. But once I recover from this, I'll eventually sort myself out and find a new job. Not another fuckin' call centre though."

"A few days of drinking? That's quite a lot. What about your poor liver?"

"Fuck my liver. It hasn't caused me any problems yet. And anyway, I can't help it."

"You seem quite drunk now and you're fairly putting those drinks away. Are you an alcoholic?"

"Pretty much. For all intents and purposes. An illness of mind, body, and soul I've been told."

"Do you go to AA?"

"Tried it. That and rehab. I wouldn't knock them, as they have helped so many over the years—countless numbers really—but let's just say they never really worked for me. I learnt some really good stuff from them, stuff about myself, but I suppose at the end of the day it really has to come from deep within me. Maybe I just don't want to give up drinking right now. I dunno."

"I understand."

"I seriously doubt you do."

"I promise you I really do. I know exactly what you are going through."

"Are you an alcoholic as well?"

"No, but I do have an addiction."

"Really? So what are you addicted to? You're not one of these arseholes who try to equate addiction to drink and hard drugs with being addicted to chocolate or something else non-life-threatening, are you?"

"No, not at all. My addiction is very serious indeed and, I must say, very life-threatening."

"So what are you addicted to then? I must say, you don't look like a junkie and actually appear quite well. Impeccably dressed too with that fancy designer suit of yours. I think you're full of shit."

"You wouldn't understand."

"Try me."

"No, honestly. It's nothing for you to concern yourself about."

"Seriously, fuckin' try me!"

"Okay then. If you must know, my addiction is to... blood."

"Blood? How does that work then?"

"I need blood to survive. Without it, I will perish."

"Are you fuckin' serious? We all need blood to survive! You talk some shit, I'll give you that."

"I don't mean my own blood. I mean the blood of other people. If I don't get it regularly it will kill me."

"You mean like donors?"

"In a manner of speaking."

"Were you in an accident or a car crash or something and you need blood from donors to keep you alive?"

Augustus raised his glass and knocked back his whiskey.

"Look, Stevie. I don't really expect you to understand fully, but for want of a better word, I am a vampire and I have been around now for a very, very long time indeed. I'm addicted to the blood of others. It is my life source. I need it. I crave it. Just like you presumably crave your dreaded alcohol. In many ways, we are very similar. Both addicts. It's just our methods of feeding our insatiable appetites differ somewhat. Yours legal, mine illegal."

A long pause. A wide-mouthed Stevie eventually broke the silence.

"First up. I might be a cunt but I'm not a stupid cunt. Seriously. Fuck away off with your silly, childish shit. I'm not that drunk, for fuck's sake!"

Augustus laughed loudly.

"I promise you, Stevie, it's all completely true. I could actually do with a good blood binge right now, to be honest. Fancy coming out with me later on for a kill?"

"Ha-ha, very funny, Mr. '*Salem's Lot*.'"

"I'm not joking."

"Neither am I. Well then, tell me this, Count Duckula. If you really are a vampire, then how come you're in this bar when it is still broad daylight outside? And I could see your reflection clearly in that mirror in the toilet earlier, too!"

"We're not afraid of crucifixes or garlic and don't sprout sharp fangs either! That's all just Hollywood rubbish you see in films. This isn't *Buffy*, you know. We are very real, though. An ancient people who originated in Eastern Europe back in the old days."

"Bullshit!"

"It is not bullshit, as you so crudely put it. Look, Stevie, why don't we have a few more drinks here and then later on, when it's dark, you can come along with me as I search for some new prey. I'll make it worth your while. I might even bestow upon you the honour of joining our very special and undying ranks. How would you like that? You'd become a new person altogether, your addiction to alcohol completely removed for good, albeit replaced with a new and much more satisfying one. I might even invite you to one of my blood orgies to meet a few friends of mine who I'm sure you'd like. You'd live forever. What do you reckon, Stevie? Does the promise of eternal life not tempt you?"

Another pause. This time even longer. The inebriated former call centre agent then spoke. "I'll go with you if you buy a few more rounds here and lend me fifty quid to get more drink later."

Augustus smiled smugly. "It's a deal."

The two men, one much drunker than the other, shook hands.

Stevie and his new-found friend shared a few more drinks and laughs. There was no more tension between them, both were now

completely comfortable in each other's company. They left
Hunter's bar before eight p.m., just as it was beginning to pack up
with more Goth kids and students, leaving the warmth and
friendly atmosphere of the Belfast pub and disappearing into the
chilly winter's moonlit night. The snow was falling quite heavily
as they headed up the Lisburn Road on a brand-new adventure
together. Stevie lit up a cigarette and drunkenly laughed to himself
as his new pal waited on him, smiling knowingly.

The former child magician was never seen by his family or
friends again.

CROWN OF THORNS

Alas, my love, you do me wrong
To cast me off discourteously;
And I have loved you oh so long
Delighting in your company...
- "Greensleeves," written anonymously in 1580

The outskirts of Belfast, Northern Ireland,
sometime in the late 1980s

The sound of the ice cream van's music resonated in the distance from somewhere within the concrete labyrinth that was the council estate. Tommy knew what it meant, and that knowledge made him sad. Another child would soon be reported missing, probably dead. Of course, it may very well have just been a regular ice cream man plying his trade, but that was unlikely. There weren't many about anymore. Not after everything that had happened. All that really bad stuff.

Tommy looked up to the grey sky anxiously, as if the heavens above were going to collapse inwards on top of him, the world ending finally, forever. He felt it in his stomach as it churned.

The boy got back on his BMX and pedalled towards the safety of his own home, the sanctuary of his bedroom.

As he cycled through the sterile, almost empty estate, Tommy thought to himself how this had been the worst school summer holidays yet and he couldn't wait to get back to his classes in a week's time. It would be good to catch up with his old mates, the ones he hadn't seen over the summer. A return to a normality of sorts. All that stuff with Tracey had really affected him. Upset him profoundly, if truth be told.

Then there was the business of the children in the area going missing, five in total. The rumours circulating around town just made matters worse, despite most of them probably being bullshit. But the incident with Tracey was very real. He'd seen it with his own eyes. An eighteen-year-old girl running completely amok, totally crazed, screaming at the top of her voice in some sort of foreign language. Attacking random people on the street, tearing up pages of a Bible, hurling blasphemies at Pastor Smith. Violently vomiting up pins, nails, buttons, and glass. And for an epic grand finale, leaping dramatically to her death from the Maginty Bridge, like the fallen angel she apparently was, her young life ending abruptly the moment her head crashed onto a large boulder below. Wasn't the Devil himself once a beautiful seraph?

Drugs were blamed for the Tracey incident, of course. Well, drugs and alcohol. And possession by otherworldly spirits. It may have been the more enlightened late twentieth century, but in certain quarters of Northern Ireland, the power of heavy-handed Puritanical superstition still held a tight stranglehold on many of the communities.

Tracey Simmons had been a bright young woman, but a somewhat strange one at the same time. A poster girl for the '80s Goth movement, she dressed like a cross between Siouxsie Sioux and Elvira, Mistress of the Dark, with her intentionally revealing black attire, over-the-top piercings, and colourful makeup. But there never really seemed to be any harm in her, passing her school A-Level exams with flying colours, and hanging around at nights with her friend Ashleigh, smoking and listening to bands like The Cure and The Smiths as they paraded around the estate with their trusty ghetto blaster in hand. No one ever could have suspected she would have done what she did on that hot early July night. The music and dress sense was one thing, but violence and suicide were a different ball game altogether and quite out of character for her.

As Tommy locked up his bike inside the wood-wormed shed in his backyard that had seen better days, he remembered how he'd quite liked Tracey. She'd always been nice to him. She had given him cigarettes on a few occasions and always smiled and chatted with him, which was a rarity for her. He felt they had a connection, that perhaps on a subconscious level they understood each other, their common misunderstood plight. He may not have been properly in love with her, but he definitely fancied her, wishing he was a few years older so she would maybe consider going out with him. He'd fantasised about being with her regularly. He was at that age. But now she was gone in the most horrific of circumstances. For good.

Tommy entered the flat where he lived via the back door, grabbed an apple and packet of Tayto cheese and onion crisps from the kitchen, slouched through the living room mumbling something incoherent to his mother, Evelyn, whom he lived alone with, as she watched a quiz show on TV, and made tracks up the stairs to his bedroom. He reckoned a little bit of Erasure might take his mind off things for a bit. By God, he needed something.

As Andy Bell was crooning in a melancholic fashion about throwing stones on hallowed ground, Tommy's musically enhanced mood was broken by the loud screech of his mother calling out his name. There was a phone call for him. It was his buddy, Jim. Tommy switched off his tape deck and went to the downstairs phone.

Jim was his enthusiastic self on the other end of the line, looking to meet up with Tommy in twenty minutes at the glen beside the estate, where they could venture into the woods there. He'd managed to convince one of the older boys that hung around the shops to go into the off-licence for him and buy him a bottle of Woodpecker cider. On top of the handful of cigarettes he'd stolen from his dad, Jimmy reckoned the two of them could get drunk and have a laugh together. Tommy was nervous about the idea, apprehensive as he didn't want to get caught drinking again, not after that last time at Beth's birthday party when he vomited all over her parents' new sofa and his own mother had to foot the cleaning bill. She'd kill him if he ever did anything like that again! Jim was convincing though, and quite overbearing too. He always was. After a few "I dunnos" and other weak efforts at excuses, Tommy finally relented and left the house to go meet his chum, casually lying to his mother on the way out that he was off to play football. She screamed after him something concerning his dinner. Tommy just grunted and ignored her.

When he arrived at the outskirts of the glen, Tommy was greeted by a smug and smiling Jim, his blond curtained hair shining in the evening sunlight that had suddenly decided to make a cameo appearance. Jim had his faithful old Adidas backpack, which also doubled for his schoolbag during term time, slung over his shoulder. He was taking huge draws of the oversized Berkeley cigarette he was smoking, trying to look like the coolest kid in town, but failing miserably with his rubbish attempts at blowing smoke rings. He greeted Tommy in his usual course manner.

"All right, Tommy lad?! What's happenin', ya wee fruit, ye? I thought you'd lost your balls and were gonna bail out on me again. Ya want me to leave you a smoke or what?"

Tommy took up the offer of the half-smoked cigarette and replied, trying to appear unfazed and just as cool. "No, fer fuck's sake. I bumped into that header John Mullan on the way over and he was talking his usual shite, the spoofing bastard that he is."

"What was the mad specky bastard saying this time, ha ha? He's not the full whack, him, ya know? My da says he has the mind of a child and that he has to wear plastic trunks because he always shits himself, ha ha. 'Member that time he told us he was riding Kylie Minogue *and* Madonna, ha ha?"

"Aye anno, mate. He was burning my ears with some shite about heading out tonight to meet up with a Page 3 girl. He's full of it, ha ha. Funny though. I mean, as if they'd go anywhere near him with his mad ginger hair and National Health glasses, ha ha. So anyway, did you get the *el cidnor* or what? Who went into the wine lodge for you?"

"Hutchy Rat went in for me, the buck-teethed cunt. Bastard charged me fifty p to do it too, *plus* a couple of fegs!"

"What did you ask that wanker for?"

"There was no one else about. But here, wait'll you see what else I got. I swiped it from the newsagent's when that auld witch Agnes had her back turned."

Jim dropped his backpack onto the grass below, knelt, unzipped it, and reached in to reveal a dirty magazine with the title *Razzle* emblazoned on the top of the front cover. The glass litre bottle of Woodpecker was in there too. As he began flicking through the lurid pages filled to the brim with young women with frizzy permed hairstyles, rather ample cleavage, and hairy bushes, Jim looked up at his friend with a knowing glee and exclaimed, "You wanna see some of the dirty bitches in this mighty fine publication, mate! Quality stuff indeed. I'll lend you a few pages of it for later sure."

"Cheers, lad. Does it have a 'Readers' Wives' section in that one? Frig me, look at the diddies on yer woman there!"

"Exactly, Tommy lad. Real women, not like that weirdo Goth girl you used to fancy."

"Here, fuckin' less of that shit, mate! Tracey was my friend, and she was nice and she's dead now anyway so it's not like she can defend herself."

"She was a fuckin' nutjob who went bananas, attacked a load of people in town and then killed herself! Knowing that rocket she was probably in a cult or something and had something to do with those kids going missing. It makes me worry a bit about you if that's the sort of girl you go for!"

"Just shut up and leave her alone. And she wasn't in a cult and didn't harm any kids, either! Why do you always have to get on like a dickhead at times, Jim?"

"I'm only winding you up, mate. Stop taking things so seriously, would ye? Here, c'mon, and we'll head up the glen and beat this cider into us. You want me to leave you another smoke?"

After lighting up another Berkeley, Jim slung his backpack over his shoulder again and the two boys wandered along the over-grown, debris-ridden grass banks towards the woods, chugging on their not-quite-legally acquired beverage as the sun began to dim in the sky.

It was overcast as Tommy and Jim entered the mass of trees, making their way along the slim dirt path ahead of them, snatches of light slipping in through the tentacled branches above. Already feeling a little tipsy, the lads were cautious of running into any adult dog walkers or such, those who could very well rumble their underage drinking exploits and report back to their parents, but alas the area seemed devoid of all other lifeforms, apart from the odd bird's efforts at song, as they journeyed deeper into the forest, joking and laughing on their merry way.

They walked for a good mile, further into the maze of woodland, both boys quite familiar with their surroundings, having shared many adventures here since their earliest years. Suddenly, Jim stopped to a halt.

"Here, mate. I need to go for a pish and a shite at the same time. Hold on a minute."

Tommy replied, "Well, you may go behind one of those trees. I don't wanna watch ye. And don't forget to wipe yer arse with a docken leaf or something, ha ha."

Jim obliged his friend, heading behind a large chestnut tree to the left-hand side of the path.

As Tommy waited for his pal to relieve himself, he glanced around his surroundings in awe, the alcohol in his system somewhat fuelling his appreciation of the sheer beauty of Mother Nature. Just as he was about to make some sort of attempt at a pseudo-philosophical comment about the wonder of the Universe, something on the right side of the path caught his eye.

This part of the forest sloped down into a hill of overgrown shrubbery and more trees, but at the bottom of the slope he saw what appeared to be an old building, perhaps an abandoned house. The ever-growing darkness of the woods did not help his vision, but as he squinted in an effort to inspect closer, he realised that it was indeed some sort of old house, complete with red brick and smoking chimney. Someone was apparently at home. He shouted back at Jim.

"Here, mate. Hurry up ta fuck, will ye? Wait'll you see this. I've just found an old house down the other side here."

Jim guldered back, "Be there in a minute. Whaddya mean, an old house? No one lives out here, ya header. Are you trippin' or on the glue or something, ha ha? I know this place like the back of my hand, and there's definitely no houses round here, just trees and shit."

Jim soon appeared beside Tommy, pulling up his trousers and buckling his belt as he did.

Tommy pointed. "If there's no houses in these woods then what the fuck is that?"

"Shit. That's a weird one, mate. I've never noticed that before and I've been up here donkeys times before. C'mon, and we'll take a wee nosey down there."

"No chance, Jim. Are you nuts? If there is someone living in there, they'll probably smell the drink off our breaths and then squeal on us to our parents or even the peelers. My ma will kill me if she catches me again, especially after that last time."

"Don't be such a wee fruit, fer fuck's sake. C'mon, it'll be fine. I've some Polo mints here anyway to keep the smell of drink off our breaths."

Tommy begrudgingly followed his mate down the slope in the direction of the building, through more overgrown grass and weeds. On the way down, Jim lost his footing, falling, and rolling down a good section of the hill, stinging himself on nettles along the way, much to the delight and raucous laughter of his buddy.

When they arrived at the bottom of the slope the house did indeed appear very old and in a state of disrepair. There was no garden or yard surrounding it as such, just more of the trees, bushes, and general woodland owned by the forest. The house was actually a cottage, the brickwork of which was crumbling, decrepit, and covered in moss, whilst two glassless windows peered out from the darkness. A door entrance was blocked with loose bricks, planks of wood, and other bits and pieces of surrounding junk. Jim spoke. "This is the back. Let's go round the front and see if we can get in from there."

"Yeah, I don't fancy climbing in one of those windows."

The boys walked around the side of the long-abandoned building until they arrived at the front. The heavily rotted wooden front door was lying wide open, inviting Tommy and Jim into its blackened quarters. The chimney smoke above rose gently into the quickly darkening night sky above.

"This is some freaky shit, mate. It's like something out of a horror film, ha ha," jested Jim.

"I know, lad, ha ha. I don't think we should go in though. Someone might be there," responded Tommy nervously.

"Don't be daft, there's no one living in there! No one has lived in there for years."

"Then why is there smoke coming from the chimney?"

"Probably just someone fuckin' about or maybe glue sniffers have been using it?"

"Aye, probably. But what if they're still there? Probably best to just leave it, mate."

"You *are* a wee fruit, fer fuck's sake! C'mon and stop wasting time, you big scaredy cat!"

The two lads entered the doorway with trepidation. The hallway was filthy with soot and animal droppings covering the floor and walls. The air inside was filled with the vilest of stenches, almost choking anyone who entered, the odour of something extremely unnatural.

The boys moved into the first room on their left, through the doorless entrance, and into a scene of unsettling strangeness. Small flames were lightly dancing from the fireplace, the sticks and coal contentedly crackling away. There had definitely been someone here at some point recently. The fire made the room feel warm but also enhanced the intensity of the bad smell to almost unbearable levels.

More soot and general dirt covered the entirety of the room, and as the boys turned to inspect the wall behind them to their right facing the window, they were greeted with the most grotesque imagery in the form of a large malevolent face. A huge, highly detailed drawing of the countenance of a profoundly unsettling being stared back at them devilishly. Almost taking the appearance of some sort of twisted demon, the face's skin was a combination of vivid yellow and black streaks, like some sort of human wasp. It had untidy black hair, elvish-looking pointed ears, and what appeared to be sharp needles protruding from its eyes. It was wearing a black Elizabethan-style ruff. Surrounding the face on the wall was a selection of messily written quotes, graffitied seemingly in coal in a near childlike manner:

MISTER NEEDLESTICKS, ALWAYS PLAYING TRICKS!
LONG LIVE THE MOON BIRDS!

"I don't like this, Jim. I wanna go home."

"Yeah, this is some weird-ass creepy shit, mate. Probably devil worshippers or something. I wanna check the rest of the rooms though. There might be something worth grabbing."

"Are you having a laugh, mate?"

"I'm not, Tommy lad. Pull yourself together, ya fruit. Two minutes, that's all. C'mon."

Jim and Tommy exited the room hastily together to check out the rest of the cottage.

There were three other main rooms. Two of them were empty, despite the same filth and putrid smell, but when the boys entered the room on the far right, they found it contained an elegant wooden table with a regally designed box on top.

As if hypnotised by its presence, Tommy and Jim walked towards the box on the table, and as they did so, it suddenly sprung open. Beautiful music filled the room as a little porcelain ballerina rose from the inside the box and circled slowly around, lifting her right leg in a dancing motion with tiny blue dancing shoes on her feet. The metallic-sounding song was one that Tommy recognised instantly—"Greensleeves"—a song he had first heard in primary school, but one that was also the same tune he had heard emanating from the mysterious, always distant ice-cream van, that in itself always seemed to be an omen of bad things to come, namely the missing children.

As Tommy became more entranced by the music box and its

song, Jim broke the tension completely by grabbing the little ballerina and yanking it off the box, tossing it with disregard onto the floor and laughing.

"You fuckin' dick, Jim! What did you do that for?"

"What's the matter, Tommy lad? You scared or something, ha ha? Ah, c'mon, mate. I'm just having a laugh. This is stupid. This place isn't haunted or anything like that. There's no such thing as ghosts. I'll admit there's probably been devil worshippers here or something like that, but they're just weirdos, ha ha. Stop taking it all so seriously."

And with that, Jim violently knocked the music box off the table where it fell onto the ground and smashed into pieces, emptying its contents across the floor. An odd-looking black egg, one that must have been hidden in a compartment at the very bottom of the box, rolled across the ground and into the corner of the room. Tommy and Jim looked at each other in confusion and then back at the egg, which had begun to crack.

As the egg cracked ever so gradually, some form of creature appeared to be attempting to clamber out of it. First a tiny, amphibian-looking finger. Then more slimy digits. Two black beady eyes peaked out from under a broken section of shell, its small head raising to reveal a dark green toad-like abomination, its gaze fixed intently on the two friends. It blinked a couple of times before jumping from its broken shell, its birthplace, and hopping furiously with menace directly towards the two young lads. Tommy and Jim let out a collective gasp and took to their heels, sprinting as fast as they could, not just out of the house but back through the trees and woods until they reached the edge of the glen beside their estate. They were too startled to ever look back to see if they were being pursued by the toad-thing.

When the boys finally stopped to catch their breaths at the edge of the glen, they took a seat on a nearby wall on the outskirts of the estate. Tommy finally broke the silence.

"We can't tell anyone about what we saw tonight, Jim."

"But we have to, mate. There's something really bad going on in that house and I think it's something to do with Satanists or something. You've heard the rumours. I bet this has something to do with the missing kids in the area."

"We don't know that for sure. I really don't think we should tell anyone at all about this. Honestly, mate."

"But this is serious, Tommy. I know I act like a dick and stuff a lot of the time, but if we don't tell someone about this then something really awful could happen, or worse: someone could get killed. Just like those kids."

"But those kids might still be alive. For all we know they've probably been kidnapped by some pervert or someone like that. I dunno, but I bet no matter what happens we get into a shitload of trouble over it anyway."

"Look, how about this: we go straight home now and say nothing to anyone, and then we meet here tomorrow at lunchtime, say about twelve o'clock or so, and then we'll work out a plan about what to do. Whaddya reckon, Tommy?"

"Okay then, fair enough. Let's just have a smoke then I'm going home to bed, and I'll see you here tomorrow at twelve."

Jim nodded.

The friends shared a Berkeley in silence before heading in opposite directions through the estate to where they lived.

As Tommy shuffled into his flat living room, his mother eyed him up suspiciously.

"Where have you been, mister? Your clothes are stinkin' and I can smell smoke off you again. You better not be bloody well smokin' again! That Jim one is a bad influence on you!"

"I haven't been smoking, I promise you. I'm tired. I just wanna go to bed here."

"You better not have been! Are you not having any supper? You didn't even have a proper dinner tonight. I can make you some cheese and toast if you want."

"I'm okay, mummy, honestly. Just leave me alone. Night night."

Tommy slumped up to his bedroom, soon clambering into bed and falling asleep almost instantly.

He dreamt heavily that night. About his father. And Tracey.

Tommy, seven years old again. At home with his parents watching Coronation Street *on TV in the living room. Loud, violent, continuous banging on the front door. His father gets up from his armchair to investigate, startled. He is wearing his green RUC uniform. As Tommy's father goes to look out of the blinds the front door is vehemently kicked up the hall. Two men with their faces covered in black balaclavas carrying AK-47 machine guns storm into the living room. The masked Provisional IRA men unload a barrage of shots into the upper head, face, and chest of Tommy's father, who drops to the ground lifeless. Tommy's mother screams hysterically. Tommy is dripping in blood as he kneels on the ground, cradling his father's lifeless body. A body that no longer has a face. Just a bloodied mess of bone and sinew. Tommy looks up at his father's killers. The balaclavas are no longer there. In their place is the demon wasp-face from the mysterious house. They have needles in their eyes...*

Tracey seated on his bed in a glorious white gown, dejected. Weeping. Taking him by the hand. Night-time outside. No stars in the sky. Complete silence. Empty streets. Frogs raining down from above. Walking slowly, endlessly for what could be an eternity but may very well be just a few seconds. At the glen. Down through the woods. Frogs everywhere. Hopping backwards, disjointedly. Into that awful house. Demon-face on the wall moving, smiling. More frogs. Toads now too. Some with two heads. Frog-toad hybrid creatures. Dark blood splattered upon the floor. Silence broken by the screams and cries of young children, drowned out by a wicked laugh from the face. Tracey speaks:

"Mr. Needlesticks, he caused all of this. He made me do it. I'm sorry. I didn't mean any of it. He controlled me and the other girls from before. So many of us. He's been doing it for centuries now. It's just a game to him. Entertainment for the delight of his masters, the Forbidden Ones. Our souls are lost in the abyss, the dark place. Help us. Save us. Tell someone..."

Tracey with a crown of thorns placed majestically on her head, weeping. Tears of blood dripping onto her white gown...

Tommy awoke.

He'd apparently overslept, but when he came to, he found his mother Evelyn shaking him from his sleep. A worried-looking Jim and his father David were also in the room.

"Come on, son, get up. There's people here who want to speak to you."

Tommy wiped the bleariness and bad dreams from his eyes.

The tall, greying David spoke next. "Stick some clothes on, Tommy. Jim told me what you boys saw last night. This could prove very serious indeed and the police might well have to get involved too, but in the meantime, Pastor Smith wants a word with the two of you. He's down the stairs waiting on you. You've nothing to worry about, though. Just be honest with him and everything will be okay. We'll see you down there in five minutes. Hurry up now."

David and Jim left the bedroom, followed by Tommy's mother after giving her son a reassuring nod and smile. Tommy soon followed them a few minutes later after slipping into his Cthulhu t-shirt and tracksuit bottoms and going into the bathroom to urinate and throw some water over his face.

Pastor Samuel Smith was seated in the armchair drinking tea and wearing his usual sharp suit, his tidily cropped dark hair on top of his usual blisteringly red face that looked like a berry about to explode. Tommy's mother had often wondered if this was perhaps caused by a secret alcohol addiction, but nevertheless, she always found him a somewhat handsome, attractive man, especially for one in his early sixties. He could be a little overzealous, for sure, during the rare occasions when she had attended one of his services, but well-meaning at the same time, she reckoned. He'd certainly been a great support to her when her husband was murdered a few years before, although she didn't appreciate the time he made a pass at her, one she soon just put down to a temporary shortcoming.

The pastor eyed Tommy closely as he tiredly slumbered down the stairs. When the boy realised he was being inspected by the churchman, he automatically straightened himself up and murmured a meek, "Hello." Pastor Smith smiled condescendingly and asked the lad to sit down on the edge of the sofa beside his mother and Jim. David remained standing, a sombre expression painted upon him. The man of the cloth lifted a plate of toast from the coffee table in the centre of the room and handed it to Tommy.

"Here, get that into you. You're gonna need the energy for what we've got planned for today. I hear you and your wee mate Jim there found the hideout of practitioners of the dark arts last night. Well done, although you're very lucky there was no one there when you found their little cesspit of activity. Who knows what they would have done to you? Jim told us all about what was there and what you were doing there in the first place."

Tommy turned and stared at Jim. Jim dropped his head guiltily. Pastor Smith watched both boys intently and continued, rather more threateningly this time, as Tommy nibbled nervously on a slice of toast. "Myself, your long-suffering mother and Jim's father here have been talking and we've decided that we'll let the under-age drinking, smoking, and masturbation slide for the time being on the condition that you return to church this Sunday. You need Jesus in your lives, boys. If you don't, then you will only spiral more and more out of control, and when you die you will be damned to Hell for all eternity. Do you know what will happen to you in Hell, lads?"

Tommy and Jim both shook their heads. Pastor Smith removed a Bible from the inside of his suit jacket and held it up, before raising his voice dramatically, sinister, to a level close to shouting. "There you will be cast into the lake of fire where you will be continually tortured by demons and witches, the filthy offspring of devils! You will experience excruciating pain like you have never experienced before and it will be continuous, your tormented, agonising screams never ceasing as your eyes are gorged out and your wretched wails only multiply again and again. But no one will listen to your pathetic screams. They will fall on deaf ears forever. A billion years is a mere day there. It's all written down here, you know, in the Word of God. The Truth. And you will never see your parents or loved ones again either. Your father is in Heaven waiting for you, Tommy, but if you don't do exactly what this good book tells you to do then you'll never get to speak to him again, and I can only imagine how disappointed he will be in you if you let him down again. So... morning service on Sunday then, boys?"

The two lads nodded, not quite fully accepting the pastor's wildly extravagant and colourful claims, more intimidated by the man himself. David and Evelyn looked disturbed and confused, but kept their peace anyway, not wanting to rock the boat.

"That settles it then, lads. There will be a great rejoicing and singing in Heaven at the news of you two young sinners returning home, like lost sheep returning to their flock. And always remember, God loves you very much. Now, let's return to the business at hand. Evelyn, could you fetch me another cup of tea please? There's a good girl now."

Evelyn did as she was told and when she returned a couple of minutes later the clergyman continued his aggressive private sermon.

"Despite your immoral reasons for being out in the woods yesterday, I am indeed very grateful for what you found there. I believe it is all part of God's great plan to rid this area once and for all of the evil that has plagued this part of the world for many centuries up until the present day. You've heard of the Islandmagee witchcraft trials, yes?"

Tommy and Jim moved their heads to indicate they did not. Evelyn nodded her head in agreement whilst David simply stated, "I have."

The egotistical pastor spoke again, as always relishing the sound of his own voice. "Almost three hundred years ago, some young girls in nearby Islandmagee were found to be practising witches in league with Lucifer after displaying supernatural powers and appearing to some of the townsfolk in spectral form. They were put on trial and jailed for a year, a grave mistake of epic proportions, of which there is no doubt. On their release from prison, they swiftly disappeared, but their curse on the town and the surrounding area has remained to this day, appearing sporadically over the resulting decades. That vile slut Tracey Simmons was one of their modern-day coven, and her death on the bridge was indeed an act of great grace from God, but we have to make sure that this insidious evil is quenched for good. We must act expediently. I believe what you boys discovered last night, this house, this den of iniquity, is very possibly the source of all the wickedness, and it must be destroyed completely. I believe when God speaks to me; He is telling me directly that this is what we must do. Some of the other men from the church will be here soon, and when they arrive, you boys will bring us forth to this house of Hades where we will do what must be done in our carrying out of the Lord's work."

The rest of the room sat in stunned silence, almost afraid to question the presence of the excessive preacher. Jim eventually spoke up.

"I don't believe in ghosts or any sort of supernatural crap like that. It's all just the biggest load of ballocks to me, made up to scare little kids at night. That's what my big brother says anyway. He told me the church is full of shit and only out to control people for their own ends. That girl Tracey Simmons was probably just out of her head on drugs or something."

Pastor Smith's face appeared to redden even more, if that was even possible, as he furiously stood up, reached over to Jim, and slapped him hard across the face, leaving a burning handprint on the young teenager's left cheek. David immediately jumped between the two of them, spinelessly apologising for his son's statement. The preacher, still seething, spat words of anger in the boy's direction, past his father.

"You wicked little bastard. How dare you question my standing with God! For it is written in first Timothy, chapter four, verse one that the Spirit clearly says that in the later times, some will abandon their faith and follow deceiving spirits and things taught by demons! But the Devil who deceived them shall be thrown into the lake of burning sulphur, where the Beast and the False Prophet have been thrown. And there they will be tormented day and night for ever and ever! David, see to your son and prepare him for the business at hand immediately. The rest of them will be here soon."

146

As the gang of four adults and two teenage boys walked through the glen, Tommy and Jim slacked back enough to get talking to each other in whispered tones.

"You're a dickhead for getting us into this, Jim. Why did you have to go and tell your da what we were up to?"

"I'm sorry, mate. But I had to. He smelt the drink off my breath and went ballistic. We'll get away with it though, trust me. All we have to do is play along and let them perform one of their crazy exorcisms on the house, then go to a few of their bullshit services and it'll be all good. Just go with the flow and this will all be over in no time," stated an overconfident Jim with a wink.

"I don't think I want to spend another second in the company of these mentalists," replied Tommy, laughing a little.

"Ha ha, you're not far wrong there, mate."

Pastor Smith interrupted the conversation from ahead. "Hurry up, you two. Less chat and more prayer. God is guiding our way. We are booking our place in Heaven today. Rejoice!"

Two other men had joined the pastor at Tommy's house shortly after his little outburst at Jim, while Evelyn had been ordered to stay at home. What they were about to do was not for the eyes of a woman, she was told. Brother Daniel was a naïve young twenty-year-old, with a polite manner about him, dirty fair hair, and piercing blue eyes. Brother Ian was a short, rotund, balding chap nearing middle age who also happened to be carrying a canister of petrol with him. It was obvious what this group from the church had planned as they ventured into the woods, singing hymns to keep their spirits up.

The males young and old trekked through the thick trees of the forest, the adults with determined looks etched onto their faces, onward Christian soldiers marching on their most important pilgrimage yet.

They soon arrived at the run-down old house thanks to the direction of the boys. The place looked different in the broad daylight, but still somehow unnatural and nefarious. It reminded Tommy a little of the cabin in *The Evil Dead*, a classic Video Nasty he and Jim had watched a few months back, but he then had to rebuke himself about how this was now real life and not some over-the-top silly horror film. He was reminded of this fact when he stared through the window and saw the malevolent demon-wasp face staring back at him from the distance. The being known as Mr. Needlesticks. It seemed to have changed since the last time he saw it. He was sure it was grinning more broadly, and its hor-rific-looking yellow-black features and its eyes with needles in them were more strikingly vivid this time, but this may have been a mere trick of the light caused by the brightly burning sun above.

Pastor Smith took the lead again. He ordered Brother Ian and David into the house as he stood outside with his arms out-stretched, loudly proclaiming the Lord's Prayer over and over again whilst Brother Daniel began singing the words to Psalm 23 at the top of his voice. It was bordering on the ridiculous. Tommy and Jim glanced at each other, both resisting the urge to burst out laughing, but as the intensity of the situation increased and the two men's rantings became louder and even more deranged, the whole scene started to quickly become very weird indeed. Disturb-ing even. David and Brother Daniel soon reappeared from inside the house with Daniel tossing the now empty petrol can into some shrubbery at the side. David lit a Swan Vesta match and flicked it into the house, the ensuing explosion knocking the four men and two boys completely off their feet.

The house was engulfed in flames, flickering and jumping on the inside and outside as the party pulled themselves back up into standing positions and stared in amazement at the inferno ahead of them. There seemed to be noises and muffled screams coming from within, the demon face in the background seemingly laugh-ing at them in mocking contempt.

Pastor Smith ordered the posse to retreat immediately and head back into the woods, which they were all more than happy to com-ply with. As they walked quickly upwards into the brown and green, Tommy glanced back and for a split second, he swore he could see Tracey Simmons on top of the roof, the flames burning throughout and over her. Her skin was blistering and charred badly, whilst she screamed a silent scream. On her head, once again, she wore a crown of thorns. Tommy speedily turned away, hastily walking from the scene with the rest of them.

There was a collective relief when they arrived back at the glen and stopped to regroup. The pastor slapped each of their backs in turn and congratulated them on a job well done. They would now go back to the church for prayer and refreshments. He told them that he believed they had been successful in their mission, although they must be ever aware as the dark forces at work could very well soon be out for revenge and they must always be on alert for the rest of their lives, prepared for the worst. When David asked him why he hadn't told them all this before, he tried to reassure him that it was a price worth paying for the rewards they would receive in the afterlife. David didn't look too convinced or happy.

Tommy and Jim just appeared deeply worried and scared. None of this was in any way a joke to them now. Jim seemed to be petrified and on the verge of tears, looking more like the young boy that he really was than ever before, his mask of bravado now fully slipped. As Tommy went over to console his best friend and ask him if he was okay, he noticed out of the corner of his eye a strange, black toad-like creature right beside Jim on the ground, hiding in the grass. It was almost exactly like the one that had hatched from the odd egg they had discovered in the house the night before, only much larger and with salivating, piercing teeth protruding from its grotesque amphibian jaws.

Before Tommy had the chance to warn anyone, the monstrosity pounced high in the air, lodging its weirdly formed teeth into the side of Jim's neck and biting down deep. The child let out a panicked scream, grabbed at the creature unsuccessfully and fell to the ground, as blood gushed from the wound and the beast let go, hopping off into the safety and camouflage of the surrounding overgrowth.

Jim wept uncontrollably in both pain and sadness. His father cradled his boy, apologising over and over again. Jim muttered to his dad about how afraid he was and that he was too young to die. David tried to reassure his son that everything was going to be okay and that he would take him to a hospital straight away. But it was all in vain.

Jim McKenzie's life slipped away from him mere seconds later.

October 4, 2022

Tommy never did get over the events of that summer back in the late 1980s. For many years he blamed himself for his part in Jim's death, perhaps a survivor's guilt of sorts, or just lamenting about what he could have done differently. But most of all he blamed Pastor Smith.

One night in 2005, full of vodka, he paid the good pastor a visit to his home with the intention of beating him to a pulp for everything he had caused with his bullshit bullying beliefs. But he couldn't go through with it in the end when he found the fake preacher to be just a weak and lonely old man. Instead, the preacher felt the full wrath of Tommy's verbal anger, telling him exactly what he thought of him and what he had made happen all those years before. The clergyman just agreed with him and pleaded to be left alone to die in peace. Pathetic really.

Now a recovering alcoholic, almost three years into sobriety, a divorcee with two children of his own that he had barely seen over the years, Tommy was finally beginning to get over his demons from the past. His mother Evelyn had passed away eight months prior, and he had made a promise to her that he would continue to stay sober and rebuild his life.

The missing children were never found, presumed long dead. Their poor families were never put out of their misery, many of them going to their own graves tormented by the lack of knowledge of what had happened to their babies.

Over the years, Tommy often dreamt about Tracey Simmons. She seemed to be at peace, and he would regularly visit her grave to lay flowers. Jim's too. He often wondered what his old mate would be up to these days had he not died so needlessly as a young boy when they were both just thirteen years old. He'd probably still be a dick, Tommy would often joke to himself.

After many years living in the Ballysillan area of north Belfast, Tommy eventually moved back to the estate where he grew up in an attempt at a fresh start and to come to terms with all that had happened in his life.

The day after he moved the last of his belongings into his new flat, he looked around his new home in a more optimistic manner. *It's never too late to change and make a go of your life*, he thought. For the first time in as long as he cared to remember he felt a glimmer of hope for the future.

He went outside his front door and lit up a cigarette. As he looked around the estate where he had spent his childhood days, he reminisced about the old times and thought of Jim and all those times they had spent together: the fly smokes, the underage drinking, the other childish—though generally harmless—nonsense.

Tommy smiled.

In the distance, he heard an ice cream van plying its business somewhere at the other end of the estate.

It was chiming out the tune to "Greensleeves."

A Familiar Rat

There is a secret room in my childhood home. It has always been there, at least for as long as I can remember. No one else knows about it, apart from the beautiful woman who once lived there and very possibly still does—the one who never seems to age.

I first encountered the room when I was a young boy of eight years old. I was sleeping soundly one night, as one does at such an age, when I was gently awakened by the sound of some very faint singing from an angelic-sounding voice, the likes of which only the heavens themselves could have spawned, whispering sweet, melodic tones directly into my mind. I suppose I was too young to fully grasp the elaborate intricacies of the dreaming world as I do now, but I strongly believe that it was all very real. I can't recall the name of the song she so beautifully relayed—nor even do I know *her* name—even though she once told it to me, but I do remember hearing it several times as a lad, siren-esque, always the precursor to seeing her again in all her radiant, nature-defying beauty.

I can, however, remember the name of her pet that would sit by her side sometimes when we met, that funny little rat-creature named Brown Jenkin, with its odd human-like face and paws, beard, and razor teeth. I believe this strange creature often spoke to me in human tongue in those earlier times.

When I first heard the woman's singing all those years ago I at first believed it was hypnotising me, almost sending me drifting off to sleep again. But I needed to pee, and it was becoming too uncomfortable to ignore, so I pulled back the blankets off my bed and made for the bathroom. It was in the landing of our house that I then noticed the secret room.

Situated on the wall between my parents' and older sister's bedrooms was a wooden door that I had never seen before. It looked old—ancient even—the wooden panels rotting at its tops and bottoms. It was slightly ajar, swinging gently from the chill of the cold breeze emanating from it, along with that soft, gorgeous voice and its song, beckoning me to enter. I thought of waking my parents to tell them about it but reckoned I would get into trouble for being out of my bed so late. My moody sister would probably shout at me and cause a whole stir, too, just like she always did, so I decided not to bother them. I could feel the door tempting me, *willing* me to open it and go inside, but it perturbed me a little at the same time, and I now needed to go to the toilet badly so quickly dashed off in the direction of it.

After flushing and washing my hands, I stepped back onto the landing. The door was still there, the dark gap where it was gently opening, inviting me to explore further, although I could no longer hear the woman's singing. I was now surrounded by an almost deathly silence.

I was noticeably sweating now, a bead of perspiration dropping onto my pyjamas top, intrigued and nervous as I approached the door to see what was lying in wait for me behind it. As I pulled it back and peeked inside, I was greeted by something that did not make any sense to me at all.

The vast, darkened room in front of me defied all known logic, not adhering in any way to the laws of physics or any other part of the natural world. It felt like I was looking into Doctor Who's T.A.R.D.I.S., but a twisted, nightmarish version of it. The architecture was all wrong. The walls, ceiling, and floor were bent and deformed, at distorted angles, like some sort of expressionist German artwork. It was dirty inside, too, filled with dust and grime, as if it had been unoccupied for a very long time, weird etchings and symbols scraped into the walls, mysterious and nonsensical lettering in some sort of alien language. The fact of the room's very existence in the first place was totally improbable. It was way too big and was encroaching well into the space where my parents' bedroom should—and in the sane, ordinary world, did—occupy. I walked further into the room anyway, entranced by my new surroundings.

When I first noticed the woman in all her garish, though somewhat regal, splendour, she was seated at the furthest end of the room in a luxurious and out-of-place large black seat (throne?), itself adorned with more of the strange, indefinable runes. She was reading a magnificent, leatherbound book, but stopped when she noticed me approaching, glancing up at me and smiling. She was the most undeniably stunning creature I have ever witnessed, her deep, dark eyes like enchanted pools you could fall into and drown, her soft pink lips and smile erotically charged and sensual, her wavy blonde hair like silk, flowing down the white flesh of her perfect hour-glass figure and more than ample breasts, cruelly concealed beneath the royal purple, tightly-fitting dress with which she was adorned so stylishly.

She asked me to move closer, her tender, elegant feminine voice proving to be irresistible, soothing, and welcoming, whilst at the same time dangerous and forbidden.

She smiled again in acknowledgment of my obedience and, addressing me by name, politely asked me to sit on the floor in front of her as she had a secret to tell me, one which I was not allowed to share with anyone at all.

I sat in silence as the woman casually relayed to me how she was my friend, my *special* friend, and how she had been waiting for me for a very long time, many years before I was born. She told me how she loved me even more than my mother did and that, in fact, in a way, she was my *real* mother, forging my essence from the space dust of the universe many decades prior on a night when the stars were right. She assured me I was a very good boy, the *best* boy, and that she would speak to me again soon when I was a little older and the time was upon us, and for me to prepare for the very special tasks she would have for me, for which I would be rewarded for in the greatest ways imaginable. She got up off her seat and bent down and kissed me on the cheek, telling me to return to my bedroom until we met again.

Everything went fuzzy after that, the woman and my surroundings gradually blurring out of focus, and I soon found myself drifting out of consciousness completely, awakening the next day in my own bed.

The years of my childhood rolled on without any major incidents, and eventually I put the whole experience down to a particularly vivid dream, probably brought on by some sort of fever I had possibly been harbouring at the time, unbeknownst to me.

I was doing well in my studies, passing my exams and attending a renowned grammar school in the city, with a promising future lying ahead. I didn't see either the woman or the secret room again until I was fourteen and by this stage had more or less forgotten about both.

It happened in a very similar manner as before: waking in bed, the song of the siren, needing to pee, noticing the secret door in the landing, and entering it. Although seven years had passed since our last meeting, the woman didn't seem to have aged at all, and if anything, she looked *even younger* and more beautiful than before. I asked her what age she was. She told me that she was much older than I was but that she had managed to hold on to her youthful looks. I then asked her what her name was. She didn't have one that I would be able to comprehend in a human tongue. I enquired as to why I hadn't seen her in so long and she responded that she was waiting for the right time. She let me know how proud she was of me and that I was shaping into a fine young man. She then explained that she was once a well-revered religious woman, a guru of sorts, the leader of a clandestine sect that existed long before all the current major world religions, their god a supreme being from the stars named Nyarlathotep, and that she and this deity had some simple tasks that they wanted me to complete for them, part of the final preparation for my *becoming*, telling me not to worry as they would be easy to complete and rather enjoyable in the bargain.

Firstly, she had a book for me to read—the very same one that she was holding when we first met—a tome connected to her old religion that contained the answers to many of the arcane mysteries of the universe. Its title was the *Book of Eibon*.

Lastly, my alluring friend shocked me by stating that she knew some of the other boys in my school had access to illegal drugs which we referred to as "acid" and "trips." She knew I was anxious and wary about dabbling with these types of substances but not to fret as it would be fine and that she would be watching over me and protecting me. These drugs would also, she informed me, open my mind sufficiently enough to the sort of cosmic knowledge that both she and the *Book of Eibon* had in store for me, and that I should try drinking some alcohol when I could, too, before eventually moving on to stronger, more powerful mind-enhancing drugs.

As she finished what she was saying and went to turn away, I couldn't help but notice that for the briefest of moments, her face appeared to suddenly change, flickering momentarily from her usual mesmerizing looks to that of an appalling, grotesque and withered visage, one with nothing but abhorrent intent etched upon it.

I obeyed both of her commands, regardless.

The next time I saw the woman was three years later, having left school early at sixteen after failing my exams and becoming unemployed.

I had passed out at a party with friends after taking too much drink and Ecstasy pills. The woman appeared in my intoxicated dream as I lay unconscious, sprawled on the floor of the flat where the party was happening, oblivious to the loud dance music and general chaos going on all around me.

She was less friendly this time, telling me that she was growing a little impatient with me as I hadn't been reading the *Book of Eibon* enough, that she was disappointed in me, and that if I didn't start to take things as seriously as I should, I would run the risk of losing out on my rewards.

It was then that she first introduced to me her human-like rodent known as Brown Jenkin, a creature she claimed was her faithful and beloved pet. If I was to adhere to all her demands, she would give up her body to me and provide me with all the carnal knowledge I could ever imagine, and more. However, if I was to continue to falter, she would get Brown Jenkin to enter my mouth while I was sleeping and claw out my eyes from the inside before eating my brain while I was still alive.

As a sign of good faith, the woman removed her dress to reveal the most heart-stopping sight I had ever witnessed in my life up until that point, lying spread-eagled over her throne, her voluptuous, perfectly formed, naked body mine for the taking, which I did there and then in an intensely profound, erotic and hazily strange experience.

I woke up in my mate's flat several hours later and the first thing I did was indulge in more drink and drugs.

I was twenty-one when the woman returned. Now living in a wet hostel, I was a jobless and directionless alcoholic and cocaine fiend destined for complete oblivion.

In the living dreamland where the woman and I co-existed, she promised me that she could save me from my worldly problems if

I simply carried out a series of new requests for her. Nyarlathotep needed sacrifices, and I was the fortunate soul chosen to carry out his work for him. The murders would be simple, she promised me, the esoteric rituals required before and after all written down in the *Book of Eibon* during the ageless time before man. Brown Jenkin would be sent to assist me with the disposing of the bodies afterwards, but if I failed to comply or do the job properly then her pet would be ordered to eat alive my parents and sister instead. Do it right, however, and I would receive rewards beyond my wildest dreams and a seat by the side of Nyarlathotep.

I am now a fifty-two-year-old man. I have not seen the woman who visited me in my youth for over thirty years now, around the same time I was incarcerated in the high-security ward of a mental health facility. The first few murders were easy, just as was promised to me, as were the graveyard upside-down crucifixions and impalements once I got the hang of them. Child's play, really. It was the sixth killing that eventually led the police to me after a partial fingerprint was found at the home of the victim. I don't think they will ever release me now. They say I will always be an extreme danger to the public, too unwell.

I think a lot about my past, my growing up, the secret room in the landing of my parents' house, the beautiful woman whom I met there, the one who told me to do all those awful things. The doctors tell me she wasn't real, a delusion brought on by my troubled mind and excessive drug and alcohol abuse. Maybe they're right and this was all for nothing, a horrendous and unforgivable waste of life brought on by a fantasy, killing for a fiction and a non-existent deity.

As I lie in the bed of my secured room in Arkham State Hospital pondering my past and lack of future, I can hear scratching noises coming from outside the window. I look outside, into the inky chasm of the nefarious night ahead, but don't see anything that could have caused it. I glance at the cosmos above and wonder what dark secrets it holds within the claws of its terrible infinity and crawling insanity. Maybe I'll find out one day when the stars are right once again.

While I settle back into my bed I hear the sound again—*scratch, scratch, scratch.*

Scratch, scratch, scratch.

It sounds like some sort of rat creature.

An Occurrence at Harmony Bridge

July 1876

The noose was tightening its grip around Crazy Sam's neck. The pressure on his throat and lungs was immense as he struggled for breath, gasping and wheezing, whilst pulling on the thick rope that was grinding on his Adam's apple, burning the flesh as it moved along it. He could feel his bowels about to give in.

The silk stream below Harmony Bridge continued to flicker past just as it always did, splashing delicately off the rocks and weeds in its path as fish leapt playfully from it and birds in nearby trees chirped gaily, the natural world oblivious to the main spectacle on the bridge on this beautiful summer morn on the outskirts of the God-fearing town of Jericho, Tennessee. The domineering mountains and valleys that surrounded the town in some ways appeared to be cutting it off from the rest of civilisation, enclosing it for its own protection. Or perhaps they were shielding the rest of the world from Crazy Sam and the cynical darkness that ran within him, and, it must be said, from the rest of the town and its hypocrisy and secrets.

Sheriff Joshua, with his impressive frame, bushy dark hair, and nicotine-stained moustache and his deputies were in charge of the hanging, with the Reverend Thomas and many of the other townsfolk—those who had formed the lynch mob which had snatched

Crazy Sam from his bed as he lay with a notorious lady of ill re-
pute—also in attendance. Old Doc Minnis was there, too, rotund,
balding, as serious-looking as always, holding his trusty leather
satchel of medical instruments in his right hand while puffing on
his clay pipe held in the other. The Reverend had said a prayer as
the baying crowd of onlookers waited excitedly with a frenzied
bloodlust for the main event. One couldn't really blame them, to
be fair.

Sam had been a bad man. He'd killed and robbed many of their
kith and kin over the years, the brains behind the robbing of several banks and small businesses with his gang of undesirables, a
rancid cancer on the reputation of Jericho, one which was about
to be cut out permanently. Always drunk, always involved in some
fight or another, the residents were finally about to say farewell to
the scum of the earth that was Crazy Sam once and for all.

After his prayer, Reverend Thomas asked Sam if he had any last
words. "I'll see every last one of you dirty, stinkin' bastards in Hell!"
came the reply.

The game was almost up for Samuel Ichabod Clemence, a man
of Ulster-Scots stock, his people (good, decent, hard-working folk,
unlike the rotten apple he had become) heralding from County
Antrim, his life spanning just twenty-five years, two and a half
decades of malevolence and mayhem.

A song sparrow perched itself on Harmony Bridge and whistled
a pleasant melody on this radiant, hot day, as the noose tightened
around Crazy Sam's neck for the final time and his mind slipped
into darkness.

October 2044

Michael awoke from a bad dream. He had been asleep on a double bed, but his surroundings were unfamiliar, his memory fuzzy.
As he looked around the room he found himself in, he realised it
was a hotel room and a rather decadent one at that, quite possibly
five-star. He was dressed in a sharp black suit and tie which he had
apparently fallen asleep in, although he couldn't recall ever owning

one like it, or—much more importantly—how he had come to be in this place and situation. Maybe he'd been to a funeral (which would account for the suit), gotten drunk, and blacked out, he mused, but had no recollection of anything of the sort. In fact, he had very little recollection of *anything* at all, including his own name.

Michael stared around the room for several minutes, trying to make sense of what was going on around him. It was night-time, he knew that at least, as a sliver of moonlight slipped through the curtains of the hotel room. Thirsty, he stumbled out of the silk-sheeted bed to the room's adjoining bathroom and drank from the cold water tap until he was satisfied. He staggered back into the bedroom area and sat on the edge of the bed, pondering what to do next.

As he sat in a confused trance attempting to work out what exactly was going on—or who exactly he was—a couple of memories suddenly struck him: He had a daughter, a two-year-old named Lachelle! He wanted to see her again so badly. He also remembered the year: 2023. *Wasn't it?*

Michael went to the bathroom again and this time ran the tap and threw water around his face. He was feeling a little fresher and decided he had to exit the hotel and get some help from somewhere—anywhere, really.

When Michael left the hotel room, he found himself in a poorly lit corridor, the décor of which contrasted profoundly with the bedroom. It felt old, decrepit, damp, and musty, the brown and cream striped wallpaper adding to the feeling that the place hadn't been redecorated since the 1960s.

A foul smell hung in the air like a diseased, soiled blanket, stale and death-like. As Michael walked cautiously forward, past the doors of rooms with odd, runic symbols scraped recklessly into them instead of numbers, he began to hear some commotion at the furthest end of the passageway. Faint at first, gradually becoming more audible, he realised it was a form of chanting by both male and female voices. Michael could not understand the words they were speaking, though, as they were in no language he had ever heard before—or could remember hearing. What language did he speak anyway? *English, wasn't it?* The repeated chants were guttural, unnatural sounding, almost hypnotising but becoming more and more clear, as Michael pressed on towards them.

Nūllus est deus. Nūllus est deus. Nūllus est deus. Nūllus est deus. Nūllus est deus. Nūllus est deus. Nūllus est deus. Nūllus est deus. Nūllus est deus. Nūllus est deus...

A semi-mesmerised Michael reached the door of the room where this drumming cacophony of sinister words was coming from. It was lying wide open, broken off from its hinges in part and covered in the runic scrapings.

Nūllus est deus. Nūllus est deus. Nūllus est—

The chanting from the room's occupants broke off as Michael looked inside, to be greeted by a sight of utter depravity and insanity, the stink from before only increasing tenfold. The walls were stained with what appeared to be fresh blood. The only object in the room, which lay in its centre, were a large king-sized bed with only a mattress on it, and on this was around two dozen naked bodies, lying randomly upon it and on top of each other. On closer inspection, as his eyes adjusted to the macabre horror in front of them and he noticed several sudden movements, Michael realised that only about half of the bodies were dead and the rest—those that were squirming and slithering around the others—were alive and feasting on the body parts of the deceased, tearing at their flesh and bones in a frenzy, gorging on them, slurping their blood, like desperate addicts who had just stumbled upon a new fix after many months of sobriety.

When Michael screamed and winced in disgust, these horrible *non*-humans momentarily stopped what they were doing and looked up at him—but they had no eyes, just empty, black, bottomless sockets from the most hellish of nightmares. They seemed to be pleased that he had walked in on them and stared at him (*through* him?) blankly, but also with a menacing, gleeful delight at the same time.

Michael turned on his heels and ran directionless back down the corridor where he had just come from. He knew he had to get outside, despite not knowing where exactly outside was—or even who *he* was himself. As he ran and ran, the corridor in the hotel soon became another one just like it, and as he rounded that one it became another one almost exactly the same, and again and again and again. The hotel was a maze and Michael was its prisoner—corridors upon corridors upon corridors, scratched doors upon scratched doors upon seemingly never-ending scratched doors, the vile chanting of the wicked beings echoing and echoing all around:

Nūllus est deus. Nūllus est deus. Nūllus est deus. Nūllus est deus. Nūllus est deus. Nūllus est deus. Nūllus est deus. Nūllus est deus. Nūllus est deus. Nūllus est deus. Nūllus est deus. Nūllus est deus. Nūllus est deus. Nūllus est deus. Nūllus est deus. Nūllus est deus. Nūllus est deus. Nūllus est deus. Nūllus est deus. Nūllus est deus...

The chanting suddenly ceased, and Michael could hear a knocking sound instead. The sound of rapping on glass, it seemed. As the banging noises grew louder, Michael rounded yet another corner of one of the corridors to now find himself in a lobby of sorts and the apparent entrance of this cursed hotel.

The lobby was bleak and desolate, a brown-carpeted reception area with an unpopulated check-in desk (*who the fuck would want to check into this hellhole anyway?*) and several worn-out sofas that looked like they had been transported directly from the mid-twentieth century. Light was bleeding in from somewhere —*daylight?*—as Michael realised where the knocking was coming from. There was a young woman—blonde-haired, slim, wearing a torn blue jacket and jeans, aged in her early-to-mid-twenties perhaps—banging incessantly from the outside of the entrance to the hotel in a panicked state of disarray.

"Come quickly, you have to come *right* now!" she hollered at him through the glass.

Michael had no option but to trust the girl and bolted over to the double doors and attempted to pull them open. But they weren't budging, despite how much he pulled and struggled with them.

"They're locked! They're fucking locked! What the fuck is going on here?"

The young woman calmed somewhat. "Step back a bit, get out of the way, old man!"

Michael did as he was told.

To Michael's surprise, she removed a small revolver from inside of her jacket and fired three rapid shots at the door, splintering the glass everywhere before kicking it with all her might, resulting in the shards smashing and flying all around the ground before grabbing a stunned Michael by the arm and pulling him outside into the world that awaited him.

"We have very little time left. You've been trapped in that place for much longer than you think. We have to move, and fast. I'll explain everything once we get out of the city."

The city?

As Michael exited the front area of the hotel, the heat and light from the sun above almost blinded him. And then it all came flooding back to him—his name, who he was, where he was from…

He instantly recognised his surroundings, but there was something very *off* about them, too.

Belfast City Centre was a mess.

As Michael and his female companion walked through the debris of Royal Avenue—the crashed and long-abandoned cars and buses, the smashed-up, looted shops, the corpses in varying states of decay strewn everywhere, the plucky rats nibbling on what remained of the human body parts—he looked ahead at the remains of what was once the City Hall, now a collapsed, half-burnt-out skeleton of ruin, the once decadent statue of Queen Victoria toppled over, disregarded and forgotten about.

"What on earth has happened?" a dejected, forlorn Michael enquired.

"I'll explain later. Everything's fucked up. Everything," replied his rescuer.

"No, wait." Michael pulled the girl back. "Tell me now. I *need* to know," he pleaded.

"Later, I promise you. It's not safe here." The girl freed herself from Michael's grip and began to walk away.

"Wait a minute, who are you? Why did you pull me out of there? What's your name?"

The girl turned around and smiled at Michael.

"Don't you recognise these eyes?"

"Why should I?"

A pause.

"Because they're your eyes... *Dad!*"

Another pause. Another smile from the girl. A moment of shock and then confused realisation for Michael.

The girl broke Michael's stunned silence.

"Welcome to Hell, Daddy-o. Your granddaughter Margot is just dying to meet you!"

As a jet-black crow swooped down from the burning sky above and landed on Queen Victoria's head, Lachelle took her father by the hand, and together they walked by what was left of Belfast City Hall and through the barren wasteland towards their future.

July 1876

Sheriff Joshua and his deputies cut Crazy Sam down from the noose. The dead body dropped onto the wooden beams of the bridge with a heavy thud that startled the song sparrow and rudely interrupted its song.

Old Doc Minnis examined Sam's remains and declared him dead.

A solemn Reverend Thomas asked God to have mercy on the soul of Samuel Ichabod Clemence and then invited the townsfolk who had attended the hanging back to the church for refreshments that his wife had prepared.

As the sombre residents of Jericho made their way back into town, below their feet on Harmony Bridge, the silk stream continued to flicker, and the fish continued to leap playfully.

The song sparrow, having now seen enough, took to the skies contentedly, sweeping up into those domineering mountains and valleys of Tennessee for a new adventure.

It was a beautiful summer morn.

This story was inspired, in part, by Ambrose Bierce's "An Occurrence at Owl Creek Bridge" and the 1961 French film version of it, La Rivière du hibou, directed by Robert Enrico, which was later featured as an episode of The Twilight Zone, originally broadcast in 1964.

THE CRIMSON TOWER

I stumbled up the winding stone steps of the interior of the tower as quickly as my feet would take me. The granite stairway seemed to stretch on forever. My legs ached, as did the back of my throat as the icy cold air struck it. I continued, struggling for breath. I could view the night (space?) sky in the heavens above through an empty window—a stunning spectacle of whirling stars and flickering bright lights: rich azure blues, vivid purples and greens, fused with colours I believe no man had ever witnessed before, all embroidered, sewn into the very fabric of this never-ending curtain of mystery and darkness.

As I plundered on up the ancient stairs, I could hear the sounds—the disgusting gurgling, slapping, and slithering—of my pursuers. They were closing in on me with haste.

How long had I been here? How many years was it now? Centuries perhaps. Would this chase ever end?

As I stopped to catch my breath and ponder my predicament once more, a black-green tentacle covered in some form of mucus wrapped itself tightly around my bare right foot. I struggled with it, panicked and desperate, kicking at it with my free foot and bending down to pull it away with my hands. It wasn't letting go without a fight, but then again, they never did.

Eventually, I broke free of the monstrous limb, and it slipped back down the stairwell with an unsettling squeal to join the rest of the denizens of Hell. I began running upwards again in my eternal quest to find an exit.

Many more apparent centuries passed as I ran up that endless spiral staircase in the tower, brief glimpses of travesties of nature always following, the resplendent view from the windows barely changing in its aura of mystique and grandeur—a masterpiece of artistry created by deities long forgotten. The timeless work of the gods for certain—but which ones exactly, I have often asked myself. The righteous ones or the malevolent, or something in between and altogether indifferent to the trivialities of humankind? I hold those thoughts once again before becoming distracted by a scorpion-like claw that snapped from around the corner of the winding staircase, missing my neck by a whisker. I continue my upwards run.

I can only presume many millennia had passed when I eventually reached the impending wooden door—my journey's end at last! But what was behind it, I asked myself—a fate worse than the one I had been enduring for an impossibly long time now?

I waited apprehensively, but time was no longer on my side.

The abominations of the eternal night were almost upon me. I could hear their awful sounds—they were *gloating* with excitement. I turned to face them and that is when I witnessed them in all their true and horrid depravity—an unholy mess of putrid eyes, claws, and tentacles, slime dripping from their every nasty limb and orifice, salivating, *hungry*—and *I* was going to be their long-awaited meal!

I opened the door. It did not budge easily, a thing untouched for aeons. When it was ajar enough for me to slip through, that is exactly what I did, slamming it tightly behind me as the horrors on the other side squealed and clawed and scratched and banged on it in frustration and furious anger. I turned away from them and faced the unknown.

I was standing on the edge of the very top of the tower. I looked downwards at the dark crimson wall of the circular building. It went on for infinity, a grandiose stone architecture that continued on and on, deep into a bottomless abyss below.

I looked up and all around me.

The scene was dazzling, magnificent. Those stars. Those wondrous colours encompassing the ichorous black eternal space, never before witnessed on any human spectrum. I was hypnotised by it all. I wanted it to take me, to be inside of me, to be a part of me, to completely engulf my very being—my *essence*. I now knew what God was, and It was right in front of my eyes in all Its divine glory.

Mesmerised to my very core, I did the only thing that seemed natural to me.

I stepped off the edge of the crimson tower and fell to my destiny.

"The only thing that burns in Hell is the part of you that won't let go of your life: your memories, your attachments. They burn them all away, but they're not punishing you, they're freeing your soul. If you're frightened of dying and you're holding on, you'll see devils tearing your life away. If you've made your peace, then the devils are really angels freeing you from the earth."

- Meister Eckhart

ABOUT THE AUTHOR

Born in 1976, Trevor Kennedy is a writer and editor based in Belfast, Northern Ireland and has been working in the genre literary field for around ten years now, although he has been a fan of all things weird and fantastical for as long as he can remember. He edits *Phantasmagoria Magazine* and its spin-off *Special Edition Series*, along with other related books under his TK Pulp imprint.

Trevor is also a radio presenter for Big Hits Radio UK and co-host of *Citizen Frame* film review podcast. His day job is a complaints handler for Channel 4 (UK). Previous employment includes work as a lithographic colour proofer, composite operator for Bombardier Shorts aircraft manufacturers, the BBC Complaints department, call centre operative, and brief stints as a security guard and industrial cleaner. He can be contacted by email at tkboss@hotmail.com.